I0743522

Book of Grudges

Dan Libman

In a totalitarian state, keeping a diary remains
the last possible conversation.
—Ernst Jünger

SPUYTEN DUYVIL

NEW YORK CITY

This book is a work of fiction. Any similarities to actual events or persons, living or dead, are purely coincidental.

"American Maccabee" originally appeared in *The Santa Monica Review* and "Three Days in Denmark" appeared in *The Beloit Fiction Journal*, both in slightly different forms.

ISBN 978-1-959556-40-4

Library of Congress Cataloging-in-Publication Data

Names: Libman, Daniel S., author.
Title: Book of grudges / Dan Libman.
Description: New York City : Spuyten Duyvil, [2023]
Identifiers: LCCN 2023013398 | ISBN 9781959556404 (paperback)
Subjects: LCGFT: Short stories.
Classification: LCC PS3612.I235 B66 2023 | DDC 813/.6--dc23/eng/20230327
LC record available at https://lccn.loc.gov/2023013398

For Ben and Madeleine,

and for Molly.

I was on an escalator in a gigantic, oddly laid out convention center, just behind Henry Kissinger who was going to the same party. He seemed happy to see me. We were both talking to someone I believe was Stephen Malkmus. Kissinger held my hand and gave me directions. I didn't want to hold his hand because he's a monster and a war criminal, and also because he is old and I worried about his hygiene. His hand was cold and slightly clammy but seemed clean.

When I woke up to pee I thought there is no way I'll forget those two things, the Henry Kissinger part and something else which I can no longer remember. Got up to pee many times and felt definitely under the weather. It hurt when I swallowed and my nose was running, all of it worse when lying down. One time I heard scratching at Madeleine's door across the hall and I opened it some, I assume to let the cat out, but it was dark and don't know if he actually left before I closed the door again.

When I got up at 7am the house was lively. Ben and Madeleine making and eating breakfast. Bright sun through the windows but I could tell it was brutally cold; the radiant heater clanged in the walls like pipes on a medieval warship. Did the Daily Mini Puzzle with Molly kind of quickly. Had a weird bowel movement with a hard edge I couldn't quite figure out. Molly walked the dog and opened the coop so I could get to school in time for office hours. Stopped at Walgreens for lozenges and also bought a Gator's Aid because I felt dehydrated. Told the cashier I didn't need a bag or receipt. She seemed to take it personally, coldly pointing to my change when it rolled into the cup. She had been very friendly to the woman in line before me, telling her she really liked *both* candy bars she was buying. The candy bar woman was also a member of the Saver's Club Walgreens wants you to join. I had to tell the cashier I didn't want to be a member first thing when it was my turn and I think because of that we had started off on the wrong foot. I also said no to contributing an additional dollar for charity, so by the time I was saying "no receipt," she pretty much had me figured out.

No one came to office hours but I got a lot of rough drafts read and graded. Went to Potbelly for lunch. Short line but moving super slowly. Waited to place order, waited to get sandwich made, waited to pay while holding warm sandwich which is the worst wait of all. Kind of annoying woman in front of me at first apologized for saving so many seats, and kept checking over her shoulder to look at her purse, which she had left in the center of a long table. She did seem to be taking more than her fair share of space. I was telling the sandwich guy my specs: Italian, regular size, wheat ("Multigrain," I was corrected), when she interrupted, saying, "Excuze? What kind of cheese did you use? I didn't specify."

The guy looked over, presumably to where he had slid her sandwich. "Swiss?"

She said, "Can you take it off and use a different cheese," which I thought was an odd way to phrase it, but the sandwich maker was not flapped at all.

He just said, "What kind?"

"Any is fine. I just don't like Swiss."

He pulled her sandwich back, nudging mine so they almost touched. Gripping the top bun, he peeled the cheese like it was the adhesive part of a sticker. The store was starting to get cold because it was ten degrees out despite—or maybe because of—the sky being clear and sunny. Turned out one of the doors was wide open. There was a sign on it that said Do Not Use which had been disregarded, resulting in a steady rush of arctic air.

"Door won't close on its own," the sandwich maker said. I feared it was me who had "used" it, but I then remembered I always come through the back door because my office is in one of the buildings behind the strip-mall. He might have glanced at me just as I had a flicker of guilt on my face, but since he was working two sandwiches and the line behind me was growing, I didn't bother defending myself. With another young man busy at the register and a third slicing avocados, everyone official was occupied and I wondered who would close the door, but then even before it actually happened, I knew who was going to be the hero. The woman stepped out of line, eyed her purse—that proud centerpiece of the ghost banquet—and heaved the broken door closed.

When she came back I said, "Thank you for closing the door."

She raised her voice slightly and said, "You're welcome," which felt aggressive, but I don't think it was aimed at me. She was making a point about the lack of acknowledgement from the employees.

We had a little chat about how the store seemed short-staffed. The woman thought it was because they had started taking orders online and that perhaps they were busier than the small number of customers made it seem. I thought that was a generous way of thinking about it and that made me appreciate her slightly. It was just the two of us at the register and when the guy cashed her out, he said, "I still got to get your soup." He turned his back to us and slit open a plastic bag of white liquid and poured it into a large pot. She said quietly to me, "Sure, just mix my soup with the old stuff. Yum."

I said, "I'm pretty sure I got your Swiss Cheese."

She went to the table saved for her friends who were still mostly behind me in line. I sat on a stool at the counter against the window because it was so bright I wouldn't need to use my cheaters to read. While the woman and I had been talking I mostly kept my eyes forward, but now that she was across the store, I risked a direct look. She was laughing with someone, gesturing at the tub of half-new, half-old soup in her hand. She had highlights in her hair and it looked like she made an effort, which was more than anyone would ever say about me. I read my magazine and made sure not to look at her again, only glancing back as I walked out of Potbelly, thinking I would wave goodbye if she was looking at me. She wasn't.

Went to Suxbux and got a short; enough caffeine to pep me up for computer lab. Veronica and Aniya were the only students who showed up to the first section because I had said students could go to the Awards Ceremony later in the day for attendance credit. I was disappointed anyone had come as I was planning to take the mandatory Illinois Ethics Exam online during class. More students came for the second section, Kenny and

LaMara, who told me they were upset with how the school did online registrations for the spring semester.

Because the third section met at the same time as the ceremony, I had told that class to go directly to the Chandelier Room, sit through the awards and get some cake. All they had to do was find me and sign the attendance sheet. The Chandelier Room was packed, about a fifth of the audience were my students from various sections. Daphnie welcomed the crowd and announced the winners, reading large chunks from the winning essays and also parts from the runners up. I remember hearing that as a teenager in Texas, she had won some beauty pageant, and my guess is she organized the essay contest just to still be able to get in front of a crowd and hold forth. She read from a binder which she held formally in front of her—no lectern—like kids on Speech Team, turning the pages in a showy manner. She began by asking people to not "Be distracted by your devices and instead, pay attention to the world around you for the duration of the...." Daphnie never said anything directly, never used one sentence where five or six would do just as well. It was how she wrote her e-mails, which I only read when I was depressed and in a mood to self-punish.

Toward the end of her performance the back row got noisy. I knew it was my class, specifically Paula and Malik. Then another girl, not one of my students, *shhh'd* and called them rude, and then Brianna, who was my student, yelled back, and then it got louder. Daphnie had to stop and ask the crowd for calm. I wondered what my role in this should be since I knew the guilty parties, but everyone managed to grit it out until the last award had been received. I got mobbed by my latecomers trying to sign the attendance sheet. Walter clapped my shoulder, genuinely happy to see me. Adam handed me a pen he thought he walked off with accidentally, but I still had mine by the attendance sheet. I didn't know if either pen had actually been mine. Brianna came up just to say the altercation hadn't been her fault and I said, I knew that and not to worry about it.

But she said louder, "That girl got up in my face." Suddenly it seemed like she might cry.

I said, "I know it wasn't you. It was Paula's fault." I didn't realize Paula was nearby, but she wheeled around and glared at me. Brianna looked at Paula and I looked at both of them and then it was over as all three of us got absorbed in a wave of eager young people heading for the refreshments. The food was better this year; instead of only cookies, the staff also served goat cheese and fig crostini, which Helen told me were for a Dean's meeting but the kitchen had made too many and gave them to us rather than throwing them out. Marla, who taught in the classroom down the hall from me, walked off with at least half a dozen on a napkin.

On the way home I called Vern to confirm our plans for tomorrow and to tell him I had a cold and to be sure that wasn't a problem. Turned out it was a problem and he said we should postpone. Said he's getting blood transfusions and something about his platelets which I didn't understand, but when I got home and reported it to Molly she asked me if he had leukemia. I said I didn't know, but I thought I would remember if he used that term. Madeleine said she made a sandwich for me but when I gave her a look she admitted she had accidentally made one with Swiss Cheese and didn't want to throw it out. I said that was really weird because of what happened to me at lunch, and then I started telling the story about what happened at Potbelly, but no one was interested. I kept saying, "Isn't that a weird coincidence? Isn't that weird? I guess no one likes Swiss Cheese."

Called for Ben and we picked up Noel and drove to the bowling alley for Trivia. Daryl and Jack already there. New bartender, not Nikki. I got a burger despite having just eaten the sandwich. Noel got pork nachos and Daryl teased him about how he eats with such precision he manages to get the last bit of nacho-doins' on the final chip and leave the plate spotless. Team did well, tied for second at the half, then had a tremendous second round and were way up at the final question, bet nothing, and won handily. Back home Noel and Ben got high in the front yard and then we four including Madeleine went down to the deBasement and watched the new South Park in the DVR. I went to bed when it ended. Molly already asleep but moved some of her pillows and asked me how we did. I knew she was sleeping so didn't bother answering. I drifted off and was disappointed when I woke up to pee for the first time and saw that it would still be Wednesday for another ten minutes.

First Candle

When the fan stopped spinning there was silence in the dark. I checked the clock but it was also dead. Got the headlamp and wood from the garage and stoked the fire in the insert stove with lots of kindling so at least we'd have heat. My phone said it was just after 4am and the recorded message at Exelon reported 33 homes had no power. Expected restore time: none. Natty texted, she also had no power, which I knew because I could see a flashlight through her windows across the creek. I had picked up Molly's habit of looking out our window to her mother's house to keep tabs on things.

Madeleine's alarm went off at 5:30am. I told her the power was out and she said, "Oh no," but was pretty calm about it. Because the house water pump is electric, I got the last mug of water from the tap and gave it to Madeleine to work with.

I said, "I can go to Casey's? Do you need anything?"

She was getting ready for an all day rehearsal at school, putting makeup on by candlelight. She said, "Water and coffee would be great."

Cursed myself for having made the offer, but at least

I would be able to use the bathroom at the convenience store. Our toilets were also on the electric so there would be no flushing until power was restored.

The tables and chairs at the front of the gas station were empty most of the day, but now they were packed with farmers in overalls and boots, loudly discussing the late frost. They weren't there because of the power; the farmers started every morning at Casey's, drinking coffee and trading notes. I had gone a couple of times with Abe, my father-in-law. From the farmers I had learned there was either never enough rain, too much rain, or the right amount of rain but falling at the wrong time.

I took as many water bottles as I could carry, then poured three cups of coffee. The cashier took pity and helped me with the lids and a cup carrier. I told her about our power failure, and she agreed it sucked. Got three breakfast bacon egg sandwiches, and then on an impulse, an apple fritter since Madeleine might prefer that. Said, "Sorry," to the guy behind me in line and he said, "No problem."

I recognized the voice. It was Hank, the man who farmed with my father-law for decades and had taken over when Abe died. I said, "Hey Hank."

He said, "Dan'el."

It seemed weird that he hadn't said anything before,

but maybe he had not noticed me. I told Hank about the power situation and that I was bringing coffee and a sandwich to Natty. I thought that would make me look like a good son-in-law. Then to the cashier I said, "I'll pay for his coffee too." She was already giving me change for the first purchase and Hank was off getting a donut so I said, "And his donut." I was holding two dollars in my hand which was only enough for his coffee, so I had to reach for my wallet and break a twenty, and I had slowed the line even further because we had to wait to see if he came back with a donut or a more expensive cruller.

Hank said, "Thanks" and by the time I was done paying he was huddled with the farmers. I always assumed Hank didn't think I was worth much because I couldn't run the tractor and needed help getting the chainsaw started, but he never let on and was unfailingly polite to me. I had hoped paying for his coffee and donut would make me seem like a regular guy, although it probably had the opposite effect.

Dropped off Natty's sandwich and went home. Madeleine and I ate by candlelight, and I had just taken my first sip of coffee when there was a whir of life from the appliances; the power was back on. The appliance clocks were blinking like newborns and the insert stove in the fireplace was blowing hot. I added more wood as Madeleine headed out the door. When Ben woke up he ate the last breakfast sandwich without asking how it got there.

In the afternoon I set up the menorah with two cheap candles from Target. When we did the prayers I called my mother on the phone so she could participate from her house in New Mexico. Ben I had to call up from the deBasement and Madeleine from her room. She was sleeping from her long day and not happy. Ben was also not happy from watching the Bear's game. It had been close all afternoon and he was taking the overtime loss to the Giants poorly. I also felt not happy but couldn't quite say why. A life not well lived? Because my mother was on Facetime she was at least a beat behind and partially because of that we kept fucking up the prayers, especially the last one which only gets recited on the first day so we weren't confident with it. Also distracting was that my mother's Facetime only showed her eyes, forehead, and her kitchen ceiling. I kept tilting my phone down to try and get her face in frame, but that's not how it works.

We had no gifts because Molly was supposed to have gotten something at the airport for the kids but hadn't, and though she had gotten home in the middle of the afternoon neither of us had gone out again. The kids seem to take it as a badge of honor that there were no presents, either because it meant they were growing up or we had confirmed their idea that their parents were incompetents, or maybe both. I assured them we'd make it up in the coming days.

SECOND CANDLE.

During my first class I left the evaluation packet with LaMara because she wanted to be the student facilitator. Jasmine followed me out saying she needed help and I spent some time in the hall on her laptop, figuring out how to get the link for her e-portfolio shared. I didn't worry about Jasmine not participating in the evaluation. She would have been positive and brought my numbers up, but anything she wrote in the comment section would have been worded so badly that it would have reflected poorly on me.

Emma Cornwall sent me a note via Facebook Messenger wondering if I would be interested in writing an advice column for teenagers for Scholastic News, where she was an editor. My first thought was: How had it taken 50 years before anyone realized I should be advising teens? Emma Messenged a sample question and said if the editorial board liked my answer I could have the gig. The question was from a high school student in South Carolina who was 16, the same age as Madeleine.

"I'm the only girl in my high school robotics team and my engineering/design ideas are often overlooked. How can I be more convincing or make sure my voice is really heard even though I'm not shy?"

Jasmine was waiting for me again at the start of my third class. I got them going on the evaluations and met with her in hall again. This time she was missing her One Card, which is what students use to access the printers and buy snacks. She thought maybe I had seen it. I checked the classroom but it was not there. I reminded her we had been through this before a few weeks back when she had lost her wallet.

She said, "I lose a lot of stuff."

I said, "But last time someone stole it? Out of your purse?"

She shrugged.

"Did you ever get it back?"

She shook her head.

"Do you know who stole it?"

She nodded.

I asked if it was someone from our class. "A student who never comes any more?"

She didn't respond, but we both knew Ashlee had stolen her wallet. Ashlee was tall and imposing, and early on she had said to me, "I really like this class. I *actually* like you." She seemed stunned to hear herself say it.

I answered, "I *actually* like you too." Ashlee had bent at the waist she was laughing so hard. That day we had worked on extended metaphors and I had given the prompt, "The campus of DeKalb State University is like a..."

Most students had gone with, "...like a city, with restaurants and stores and hotels..." Or "...like a carnival with sports and games and....,"

Ashlee had written, "DSU is a strip club." She had made a pretty convincing case, talking about students spending stacks of bills and professors on poles; in her construction it wasn't even a simile. Since then, Ashlee's attendance had been spotty and when she was in class she was sometimes outright hostile, but because she had shown me that brief flicker of warmth, I was permanently in her corner. She had not turned in her final assignment but I was giving her a C anyway. The class was "developmental" and students were encouraged by the university to take out loans, so I never failed anyone who made even a slight effort.

Jasmine and I went to the English office where Richard May and the secretaries emerged from their various corners, eager to help. Everyone was being solicitous and told her it would be all right, partially because of the season, partially because Jasmine seemed helpless, and partially because she was pretty.

Ben came up to light the candles when I got home after my night class, but Madeleine was already sleeping. It seemed dumb for them to have waited for me but not have Madeleine around, and we had no gifts anyway. When we finished the prayers, Molly and I went into deBasement and watched dumb TV while Ben walked outside in the cold with his headphones on. The candles were just bottoming out when we went to bed, wispy smoke columns over the menorah.

Third Candle

Molly's mom came over for dinner with Noel, our nephew, who was living in Natty's basement. He was supposed to stay for the summer, but summer was now going into its 19th month. He was actually a steady presence in the house, and Molly was glad he was there, especially since her dad died. Doting over Noel gave Natty something to do. She made sure her fridge was stocked with beer he liked and packed a lunch for him when he went to work as a carpenter's apprentice. I wouldn't have left Natty's basement either. He and Ben were good cousin/pals and Noel was good on our Wednesday night trivia team, filling our "Manga/Anime" hole. Tonight Noel told me Dom would be stopping buy to pick up weed Noel had.

Molly bragged about the advice column for Scholastic News and everyone started asking me questions, none of which I could answer. Everyone had the impression I already had the gig and it seemed like too much effort to set the record straight. After dinner we lit the candles. Ben and Madeleine seem sort of proud and maybe a little performative to be using Hebrew in front of Noel and Natty, even if the Hanukah prayer is the extent of their knowledge. Madeleine gave me a great shirt, a flannel, just the sort I regularly wear. Molly gave me breath mints and claimed to not mean anything by it. Ben talked about his community college religion class, about how Zoroastrians were the first real Abrahamic religion.

Natty said that in church she learned Christianity has, "An underlying theme of loving your family and doing good in the world." And she asked, "Does Jewish have the same thing?"

I considered the myriad ways one might answer and finally chose, "No."

The plates were cleared and cards shuffled for Oh Hell, and after a few rounds it was Mel who showed up instead of Dom. She sat down and we dealt her in. I got her a Guinness and she broke off a small piece of a Hanukah cookie but didn't eat the rest of it. Mel grew up in the cornfields of Kansas but in high school had worked at a JCC daycare and enjoyed it, making her one of the few people in Hoogler County who knew what Hanukah was, and one of the very few non-Jews I ever met with any positive feelings towards us. Mel asked if we made latkes and when I told her we hadn't, she seemed confused. She looked tired and told us about her broken finger and a story about some of the kids fighting at school. Ben and Noel went outside to make blunts so Natty wouldn't see, which is when I realized we had been using Ben's lighter to light the Shamash. It had a marijuana leaf etched into the handle. Mel took her purse and presumably got the weed for her and Dom, then headed home. Madeleine and I sat down at the computer to work on the response for Scholastic News. We worked on it together, reading it out loud to each other, cutting, adding, altering.

I had the opening: *The first thing I want to tell you is that I am glad you're not shy. I am also not shy, and over the years I have come to see not being shy as almost a superpower. Not being shy means you're going to do great.*

The rest of the ideas were Madeleine's, which we worked out together: *But that doesn't help you with your Robotics team today. It's difficult to balance what people expect from girls, being kind and unassertive, with being heard and taken seriously. Being consistent is the best course of action: presenting yourself with confidence and being exactly who you are. If the boys don't respect your contribution, then you shouldn't care if they find you aggressive for asserting your opinions. Make a game of it and in the long run you will become a stronger advocate for yourself.*

Madeleine pointed out I had used a comma splice. I had to ask her where. "I'm horrible at my job," I said, trying to be helpful.

Once she pointed it out, I told her truthfully that I knew the comma was misplaced and probably would have caught it while proofreading, but I never would have been able to explain why it was a "splice." I wanted to tell her that my real strength was getting my "at-risk" students to show up to class and remain engaged, but then I remembered Ashlee. She was the exact kind of student I was supposed to be reaching: lots of potential, underserved by her secondary education, and she *actually* liked me. Ashlee's disinterest in her English class was a fairly damning indictment of my value.

Madeleine asked, "Are you and mom getting us anything at all this year?"

FOURTH CANDLE.

I walked from the parking lot to my office in Kernel Hall behind a guy I regularly see in the elevators. We were too near the building for me to pass him and not look rude, so I slowed to his pace. He had a bright knit cap and I thanked him when he held the door open for me, and thanked him when he held the second door, adding "again," which made us both chuckle. A woman in a puffy coat carrying several tote bags had already hit the call button so the three of us walked on to the elevator together. The guy stood by the panel and asked, "Ten?"

He and the woman were on a first name basis and both going to the seventh floor. She was holding a giant pastry box of Christmas cookies for her students.

I said, "Those look like good cookies," which I normally would not have said but I was a bit shook that the guy knew which floor my office was on.

She said, "These are the best," and added the name of the bakery.

The guy said, "Yum! You're torturing me!"

She said, "You have to be nice to your students at Christmas."

I said, "Better than Oreos," which no one replied to because it was already a beat behind where the conversation had gone and also did not make sense.

Only Paula Treelo and Malik Dean showed up for my 2pm class because they had not yet turned in their E-portfolios. Paula and Malik had a sweet relationship which I felt proprietary about because it seemed to have developed in my classroom. They often arrived late and talked to each other while I lectured, but they turned in assignments and generally paid attention, by which I mean: laughed at my jokes. Paula had wild frizzy hair and Malik was tall with a diffident mien, as though he was just barely putting up with me. As they headed out the door, Paula wished me a Merry Christmas. She said, "We got your class next semester, Libman."

Some students called me Mr. Libman, some Professor Libman, and a few mistakenly said Dr. Libman which I would correct, but only once. The confusion had to do with the fact that I don't project much authority and am myself unclear on what I should be called. Paula smartly avoided the whole issue by only ever using my last name. I liked the way "Libman" sounded when she said it, accenting the "ib" instead of the "min."

I said to them, "If you two got married and Paula changed her name, she would be Paula Dean."

Paula made a face. "He don't even like girls!"

Malik said, "Don't be putting my business out there."

Paula said, "Everyone knows." She looked at me. "Right? Don't everybody know?"

The "Personal Narrative" Malik had written for the class was about telling his mother he was gay. It had been peer reviewed by fifteen students and had taken second place in the Diversity & Togetherness essay contest. The essay was headed for publication in the next edition of the student anthology, Progressive Voices.

I said, "I didn't mean you are getting married, just *if* you did *and* Paula changed her last name, she would be Paula Dean."

When I got home at 5:30pm the world was pitch black and everyone was in the deBasement. As happens sometimes, the disappointment at my return was palpable: Ben went upstairs, Madeleine harrumphed that she wanted to be left alone. We lit the candles and I handed out index cards with presents I would get them later. A knit hat, I wrote for Ben, thinking about the guy in the elevator. For Madeleine I wrote, "Fancy cookies from good bakery." I added, *I owe U*, on both, and when they politely thanked me, I felt shame.

Took Ben and picked up Noel and headed to the bowling alley. Got the corner of the bar and Nikki gave us this week's "Football Pick'em" sheets and food menus. The bowling alley offered so few items we pretty much had the menu memorized, but we gamely glanced down the list, hoping to find something new. Nikki got my Guinness, which she pronounced "Gen-ness," as though it rhymed with "Dennis." She got Noel's Pretzel City Amber and Ben's water. Daryl was supposed to come late because of Haley's middle school Christmas Concert, but he showed up before the first question, saying the auditorium had been too crowded. "Not even standing room," he said, and Nikki put a Blue Moon on a coaster for him.

The place was almost empty for some reason, just us, Shaken Bacon, Smarty Pants and The Moops. We were way ahead at the half, which is when the Shaken Bacon guy with the smart-watch showed up. I made a loud joke about it not being remotely suspicious when Team Shaken Bacon got a question about Debra Messing correct, and people at the bar laughed, although Matt paused before asking the next question in a scoldy way. I actually didn't contribute much, in fact had argued against two correct answers. We ended up winning through smart, conservative betting and doing Ben's Sun Tzu trick on the final question. We got a "Victory Round" which took some time because Nikki was outside vaping with her boyfriend when the game ended.

FIFTH CANDLE.

Woke up in the middle of the night feeling bad about my lackluster Hanukah performance. Couldn't get back to sleep, although could have been that extra Victory Round beer. Told Madeleine in the morning Hanukah was officially back and we would make latkes for dinner. Got online and ordered books, making sure they were Prime so we could get them by the final night. Drove to Target. Got a Yankee Candle for Madeleine, weight lifting gloves for Ben, and a yoga mat for Molly. Stopped at Vitamin Shoppe thinking I could get protein powder for Ben but there were too many options. Went to the fancy bath place where the saleswoman worked me over pretty hard and I ended up with a basket of bath stuff for Molly and another one for Madeleine. I used a credit card and "signed" an iPad at the register with my finger.

The saleswoman said, "The receipt was texted to phone number ending in 3110."

I said, "That's my wife's phone."

She said, "Is that okay?"

I said, "This is a gift for her."

Another woman behind the counter squinted at the register. "We've run into that issue before. You can tell her she's got a five dollar credit on her next purchase. That part will be a surprise."

Went down the block to Rockford Art Deli to buy Ben some 815 shirts to match his tattoo but they didn't open until noon, which was still 40 minutes away. Sign on the door said, *Sorry, You Blew It. Closed.* It made me angry, and I shouted back to the door, "No, you blew it!"

In the mailbox was a mound of catalogs and solicitations, including one to Thelma McNair, Molly's grandmother who had built the home we lived in. It was from Habitat for Humanity and on the back flap it asked, "What have we done wrong?"

Lots of things, I thought. For one, taking such a passive-aggressive tone toward a woman who has been dead for 25 years.

Molly called to tell me she told her mother we would go to her house at 6pm for soup and sandwiches. I told her we couldn't do that because Madeleine and I were reclaiming Hanukah. I put the phone on speaker and walked to Madeleine's room for support.

"You're on speaker phone," I grandly announced to

Molly. And continued, "Madeleine, your mother wants to know when we should go to grandma's for dinner. I've already told her *we're* making latkes."

"High school band Christmas concert tonight," Madeleine said. "Remember?"

"So then 6pm?" Molly asked over the speaker.

Ben melted the bottoms of the candles with his weed lighter before putting them in the menorah. We lit the candles when Molly got home and like yesterday—though everyone was in a sore mood—they took the prayers seriously, recited them sweetly. We passed the shamash back and forth now that there were enough candles for everyone to light one. I gave a bath bomb to Madeleine, the yoga mat to Molly, and the weight lifting gloves to Ben. He actually seemed to light up when he saw them and started talking about his workout. Went to Natty's for dinner and then I drove Molly and Natty to the concert. Ben refused to go.

In the seats before the show I checked email. Emma Cornwall wrote that as a freelancer, Scholastic News needed me to fill out a vendor form before they could even consider looking at my response. She also said I needed to send a photo with a bunch of requirements having to do with pixels which didn't mean anything to me, and I had to set up an account and would need to submit a tax form and scan two forms of ID. I would need to use the difficult scanner at the Cole Ridge library and it all just seemed like a lot of work. As the band broke into Hot Chocolate Express, I wondered how the young robotics would have handled it.

Sixth Candle.

Madeleine's laugh woke me at 6:50am. Ben was about to lift and was still buzzing about the gloves. We four did the NYTimes Mini Puzzle and stumbled off the blocks but still got it done in 90 seconds. Walked dog. Fifteen degrees but sunny and not unpleasant. Opened coop. Busted the ice out of the metal bowls and filled with water. Napped in the afternoon for 90 minutes. Deep sleep. When I got up, first thing Molly told me was her mother would bring the apple sauce and sour cream. I had insisted we do latkes tonight which Molly was against, citing the oily mess. This was her way of saying though I had won, my victory would be pyrrhic.

It turned out that Madeleine was not really into making latkes either so Molly and I fried them ourselves. Drank a beer. Natty came without Noel. I realized that when we eat with Natty I tend to pick those days to be the ones where I don't drink, trying to demonstrate moderation. But that is exactly the wrong approach. I should drink more when Natty comes over, not less.

We lit the candles. I gave Natty some tea I had gotten for Molly, so that Natty would have something to open. I was impressed by my nimble thinking, which I attributed to the beer. Molly's bike helmet came from Amazon but I was holding it for the last night, for the big finish, so she got nothing since I had given away her tea. I gave Madeleine Casey's gift cards so she could get gas when she goes to her cello lesson, but it didn't mean much since I pay for gas anyway. For some reason I thought using the card would be fun for her.

SEVENTH CANDLE.

Drove to Rockford after chores and almost ran the red light in Cole Ridge, which I had never done before. Didn't see it change and got a car length into the intersection before noticing, stopped, and reversed back to the line of scrimmage. No one honked but weary looks were exchanged through windshields.

Molly and I were meeting the Wilders for beer—me at 6pm and Molly no more than an hour later, when she got back from doing yoga in Madison. I was looking forward to being at the Oasis which is my favorite kind of bar: dim, no TV, lots of rotating beers on tap. I reminded Beau it had been a year since I saw him on the Outdoor Writing panel, because I had just read about it in my diary. Claire had put some effort into her appearance, eyeliner and a sort of hippy outfit that an actual hippy couldn't afford. When Molly showed up, suspiciously at exactly 7pm, she was in a winter hat and a flannel, same as me. We pretty much looked the way we did when Madeleine asked us not to hover around her at the Music Academy because we "looked like hobos."

I was drinking some hoppy beer from Cali with a high ABV while Beau was jumping around the taps, trying different beers. Part of why I stuck with one beer despite all the choices was because Beau was an inveterate sipper of other people's drinks. He was tall with a long wingspan and often reached for someone else's glass without invitation or warning. His entitlement was offensive, but somehow the length of his arms—his efficiency—made it worse.

Beau mentioned Hanukah to me right off the bat, making a few jokes early on, like "Hey Libbers, you sure beer's kosher?" He demonstrated comfort with my being Jewish by bringing it up a lot. I take the opposite tack, like when I'm with gay friends, I will go to great lengths to avoid any subject related to sexuality or gender, which probably makes me seem like a prude, when actually I'm just afraid of saying the wrong thing. I assume people think of me the same way I think of myself: short, physically unappealing but funny, an adult who regularly mixes up his left and right. It's startling to be reminded people also think: Jew.

We ate gyros and chicken wings delivered from Uncle Nick's, and once the bill was paid and the paper plates cleared, we headed out. Beau and Claire wanted to see the yoga studio, so we crossed Kishwaukee and Molly used her key to open the Pranayama door. At first she tried to dissuade us by saying we'd need to remove our shoes but when that didn't work she said we needed to be quick. For Molly, the entire evening was under protest: she had asked me to postpone with the Wilders when it turned out she needed to go to Madison during the day. I had refused because it would have been embarrassing. Claire got on the ropes right away but Molly coaxed her down and got her to wrap a blanket around her hips and do it properly.

Molly and I drove home in our separate cars. I gave her a head start and she was long gone by the time I turned left on State, but I caught sight of her taillights on

Prairie, passed her just outside of Cole Ridge, and was well ahead of her coming up our driveway.

Madeleine was out having dinner with Speech Team but pulled into the driveway just after us. Ben was already asleep but Madeleine had done well and was upbeat when we lit the menorah. I decided to wait for Ben tomorrow and give all the books together, so I gave Madeleine the Yankee Candle and Molly the bike helmet. Molly stiffened after pulling off the wrapping paper, and after some denials, admitted she didn't like the color, which was all white. I was surprised to actually feel hurt. I told her I would return it and she gave me the box back. It was only later when I realized her response might have had something to do with the Wilders in the yoga studio.

Final Candle.

Vivid dreams but all that remained was the idea that I was traveling somewhere in some kind of truck-like vehicle, making a deep rut in the snow. That wasn't even what the dream was about but for some reason it was all I could remember.

Brought in wood and added to the fire. Fingers and

palms completely studded with slivers, but worth it. I love the way the fireplace becomes the center of the house when it is cold. Hearth and heart must be the same word, I'm not going to look it up. Everyone gravitates to the flickering heat, the ecstatic light. Sophie owns the rug just in front of the fire. Molly moves all the wet coats and hats into its vicinity. Ben and Madeleine stop in front of it without thinking on their way to and from the kitchen. I put tin bowls of water on the stove to keep the house from getting too dry.

On the last night we did the prayers and said the extra one because we weren't sure if we were supposed to. I gave out the books I had ordered and everyone was nice, even Ben acted enthused when he opened the hardcover copy of Paper Lion. "It's a football book," I told him helpfully. "I met the man who wrote it."

I wanted to tell him about George Plimpton but Ben only said, "Neat."

Madeleine opened her book about sushi rolling and Molly asked if I remembered she had already read Jean Brodie. "I'm the one who recommended it to you."

I broke out a bomber bottle of Stone "Enjoy By" beer and four 5oz glasses and we killed the bottle, mostly Ben and me. Madeleine and Ben had a warm conversation about speech team.

Natty came for dinner and even managed to hold the conversation at one point. At the Al-Anon potluck she had gone to, Betsy Pearson brought a "vegetarian dish" which was so bad, Natty said, "I just pushed it around my plate with a fork."

I pointed out that since "anon" was short for anonymous, Natty shouldn't tell us who was at the meeting. That was deemed such a cute comment that it was repeated to Bridget when she called later, as was the story about Betsy Pearson's dish. I realized part of Natty's scorn had to do with the dish itself. In this farming community most folks raise beef cows or grow feed for cattle, and while it would have been fine for Betsy Pearson to have brought *vegetables* to the Al-Anon potluck, labeling her dish "vegetarian" was too provocative for the family and friends of local alcoholics.

Once the candles burned down, I scraped wax off the menorah and put it back into the sideboard. The Bears game started and Ben and I watched it in the deBasement, me trying not to be annoying and ruin his good time by asking questions. I had raised him on the White Sox and baseball but he had found a measure of independence through football. Appeasing the football gods, not doing anything that might jeopardize a Bear's victory, was his religion; and on this last night of Hanukah, the Bears pulled off a miracle against the Rams.

At the two minute warning, with the game still on the line, Madeleine came down and said the slats under her bed had fallen again. Ben asked her to wait, but I went up to help anyway, finding I wasn't as invested in the game as much as spending time with my kids, who were very nearly fully grown and about to start lives which would include me only occasionally, and even then as obligation. Here was one last opportunity for me to be useful. I hoisted her mattress up while she picked up the slats that had fallen and slid them into place. When I lowered the mattress we thought we heard a slat drop, but neither one of us had the heart to check. "Don't worry," she said. "I can still sleep on it so long as most of the slats are in place." She was trying to make me feel better; we both knew a better dad would have fixed the bed years ago.

Got into my bed next to Molly feeling like I wasn't even remotely sleepy. Listened to Ben leave the house to smoke his Victory Bowl—he had told me he was also prepared to smoke a Consolation Bowl depending on the outcome.

I caught the light by my window. Ben was on the side of the house using his flashlight. I already had my earplugs in, but I reached over and raised the blinds about an inch so I could see out. I saw Ben's silhouette against the pine trees, the flicker of his weed lighter, his face in the orange glow of the pipe before fading, dark shadows, dark on dark. Nothing. And then a few seconds later the little dot reappeared, glowing orange. A festival of light.

Darkness came early with the gusting wind. Ice pellets ticked against the window and piled in dunes on the windowsill. From a cone of kitchen light we could see a mound of snow accumulating on the bird feeder like a Cossack's hat. It was Saturday night, and the four of us were going to have dinner across the creek with Natty and Noel. The snow was already too deep for the Prius so Ben and I walked down the driveway to get the pickup truck in the barnyard.

We had no trouble getting down the hill until we reached the bottom where the drifts had blown so high snow spilled into our boots—or at least my boots; Ben had on gym shoes. Other than the wooden mailbox post, there was no sign we were crossing the road as we jumped and stomped our way to the pole barn. The number pad which raised the garage door was iced over, so I took my gloves off and dug for the hidden key to unlock the storm door. Ben watched impatiently. He also wasn't wearing gloves or a coat. Or a hat.

Inside, it smelled of motor oil, dust and stillness. The pole barn was vast and held all the tractors and farm machines: the bailers and hayracks, the spools of fencing, several rolling tool chests with drawers of ratchets and sockets. When the fluorescent lights warmed up, we could see the plow had not been remounted to the front of the pickup truck. It had been removed by my nephew Noel, who had used the truck to bring his stuff to Milwaukee where he was moving from his grandmother's basement. Rent was going to be free in exchange for maintaining the upper floor Airb&b, but Noel hadn't been paying rent at Natty's, so this was at best a lateral move.

It was not difficult for one man to mount the plow, unless that one man was me, which was why I had brought Ben. Despite being my son, Ben had embraced tattoos and weightlifting, and was a surprisingly good problem-solver. He braced himself against the coupling tower while I inched the truck forward and wiggled the joystick controlling the blade, hoping to hear the clang of spring-loaded clamps locking into place. After one failed attempt, a competent person would inspect the coupling and see what had gone wrong, adjust the angle of approach, and make it work. There have been times when I struggled for hours, but this time we got it on the third try, and I was able to raise the blade in victorious salute. What we couldn't do, once we got the rolling door open from the inside, was drive the truck through the steady, cinematic snow shower. Ben texted Molly and Madeleine to walk on their own.

"Guess we're no Cap and Almanzo," I shouted to Ben as we trudged up Natty's driveway. "Remember? The Long Winter?"

The Long Winter was Laura Ingalls Wilder's best Little House book, and possibly the greatest fever dream ever written about the season. One morning it snows so much it weighs down the heads of all the cows. The entire herd is trapped, necks bent, heads buried in the snow. Only their ribcages moving indicate they are still alive and struggling to breathe. Cap Garland and Almanzo head out across the plains on a team of horses. They keep falling through the snow because the prairie tallgrass made drifts over pockets of air, but they manage to get grain and save the town. And here Ben and I couldn't even pick up Molly and Madeleine with a four-wheel drive truck.

They had arrived before us having walked across the creek in Muck boots and climbed over the gate to Natty's driveway. We toasted Noel good luck in his next chapter. I hoped we could walk in our tracks on the way back, but our footsteps had already completely filled and were no help. Later in bed I reminded Molly, "We talked about maybe doing something tonight…"

Molly said, "I know. We need to get to it soon," and then she went to sleep.

Madeleine woke me Sunday morning by shouting from her room at 4:30am. She was on the schedule to work the door for a Power Up volleyball tournament. Madeleine and I had a deal: I would plow our driveway and if the roads had already been cleared, she could go. Molly was still in bed, hadn't even been woken by the shouting, and I felt some resentment, but it lifted as soon as I walked into the dark morning. I felt lucky. Despite the sliver of moon, rivulets of moonbeams ran over the snow. I was warm in full Walls coveralls, Carhartt hat, balaclava, thick gloves and Muck boots. The snow on the road meant I was here before the township plow had cut anything open. Everything was silent in the barnyard and the drifts of snow shimmered like they had been poured thick from a pitcher.

Was that a fresh observation? Was it even possible to describe *snow* in a new way, four billion years after the formation of Earth, 600 years after the printing press and one hundred years after James Joyce wrote The Dead, the story which ends with literature's greatest description of snow? I tried to remember it: *Snow was general all over Ireland, falling on every part of the plain,* blah blah blah, *Bog of* something something *mutinous Shannon waves…. Upon all the living and the dead.*

I was disappointed in myself—not for misremember-
ing the line, but for recalling its existence at all. Being
unsuccessful at writing, I spent a lot of time assuring
myself about its uselessness. It was disconcerting when
a line from literature bubbled up, clicked, and comfort-
ed. Proof that art *could* be meaningful, but that I was just
not good at it.

We had left the door unlocked last night. The only
heat source in the pole barn was a potbelly stove which
had not been used since my father in-law, Abe McNair,
died the previous year. He liked to come down and get
the oven going with random twigs and chunks of wood
from the splitter, which he called "squaw wood." Abe
kept an old dining room chair and hid out when Bridget
visited with noisy grandkids. Natty, a former kindergarten teacher, thrived on chaos. Abe, like many farmers,
had been a teacher during the school year, but he had
gone the guidance counselor route since there were fewer places you had to be.

The big door groaned when I hit the switch to raise
it and I could hear the ice cracking in the seams. After a dismaying shudder, the motor rolled the door into
the ceiling. The cab of the pickup truck smelled like
bodywash and weed from Noel, and I raised the plow
and headed out. The snow was deep, but in four-wheel

drive I managed to plow around the barnyard, just two blade widths to the dumpster, wide enough so Hank could get in with his pickup later. Hank was particular about where the snow got pushed—he didn't like being blocked from the corncrib and needed access to the lean-to next to the barn—so I gave him just enough room to get in and finish it the way he wanted. I plowed once around the milk-house so I could throw a bale of hay to the horses later. I took a pass across the road, past the mailbox and up my driveway.

My headlights swept the distant tree line, the sky so filled with stars, *they seemed to overlap.* I was disappointed with myself again, especially for remembering that particular lyric from scoldy rock band 10,000 Maniacs. It's one thing to recall James Joyce, but it's been thirty years since I've even thought about that band. Plus, it's an ugly lyric: stars don't overlap, that would just look like a bigger star. Bad poetry disserved a stunning night sky such as this.

I made two passes up my driveway, past the chicken coop, pushing the snow into large banks near my garage. In order to move the Jeep into the now empty space, I dashed into the kitchen to get the key. Madeleine was pouring tea into a thermos. She said, "I need to go now."

I said, "The township hasn't plowed the road yet. Plan B?"

We didn't actually have a Plan A, but last night I told her if the roads weren't clear when she had to leave for work, I would drive her into Rockford, then come back when her shift was over. Before she got her license I had driven her places all the time and it sounded like fun to me—we could talk and listen to music—but Madeleine hated the idea. She had potty-trained herself at 16 months and as a toddler had insisted on holding her own hand at the edge of the Grand Canyon. Having been independent from about the time she left the womb, she wasn't going to let her dad pick her up after work, not when the state of Illinois had licensed her to operate a motor vehicle.

She said, "What about the plan where you walk home from the highway?"

I had also floated the idea of getting her to the intersection of Town Hall Road and Highway Two, where, if the state had cleared the highway, I would get out and she could drive the rest of the way herself. This was an obvious bluff since it left me walking home on unplowed country roads over a mile, but the flaw of my strategy was that it relied on teenage empathy. A better parent would have just said, No.

Madeleine and I buckled in. The Jeep hesitated when I hooked to the right out of the driveway, but I gunned it through the powdery slop and the four-wheel drive ground into action. We fishtailed some, especially as we started up the hill on Town Hall, but Madeleine was unconcerned and continued putting together her commute's playlist. With the brights on I could avoid high drifts pretty easily and by the time we reached Highway Two, we could see the state had indeed already cleared and salted all four lanes. I tapped the brakes though we could have slid without penalty—we were the only vehicle on the road.

"Keep it in four-wheel drive," I told Madeleine. "Go slow. Give yourself a lot of room to brake."

"Where is the dongle?"

A-Punk blasted through the closed windows as she turned on Highway Two, heading north to Rockford. I watched until the taillights disappeared.

It was a long walk to get home in the dark, but I felt fine about it, lucky to be the only one awake in this unmoving, snow covered world. Walking was easy in the Jeep tracks, and I focused on the distant, inky tree line and the glorious profundity of stars, which *did not* look like they were overlapping. On the contrary, each was a distinct, crystalline pinpoint. Perhaps the lyricist for the 10,000 Maniacs had an astigmatism. We're actually part of those stars, a notion that made me shiver. People needed an origin myth so they made up Adam and Eve, invented a creator God, and I've heard people say those are beautiful stories, although I never thought so. In the song, Spaceship, Kesha says we are "…nothing more than recycled stardust and borrowed energy." That actually is beautiful, and has the added benefit of being true.

A sudden orange glow lit the sky as I neared the barnyard. The township plow had finally arrived, festooned with so many whirling and spinning lights it looked like an alien carnival coming up over the ridge. Stepping out of its way, I waved as the plow snarled past, violently clearing half the road on its way toward Natty's house. The township owned the bridge on Natty's driveway, so they plowed the road across the creek, then the trucks backed up like a kitten crawling out of a narrow squeeze. *Beep beep beep…* Until a few years ago, the township would plow all of Natty's driveway since it was easier to go to the top of her hill and turn around on the teardrop in front of her house. But that was when Abe McNair was still alive and an elected Township Trustee. He worried it would appear that he was getting preferential treatment and asked them to stop. Then he died and now the township cleared to the end of the bridge, and left the rest for me.

Inside the pickup truck, plow engaged, I considered

petitioning the Road Commissioner to clear Natty's entire driveway, but since the hotly contested election of '18, he was unlikely to agree to it. The Road Commissioner of 30 years had been beaten by an upstart, someone from the corner of Rockvale Township across the river, and I myself lost my bid to keep Abe's trustee seat in the family. I came in sixth place out of six people vying for five seats. I didn't just lose, I was *the only* person to lose. Usually township residents had to be recruited to fill the seats, and no one had lost an election in such a long time, the clerk had to look up the rules. My loss involved a mandatory recount and an official notice in the newspaper. The election went over budget, giving me possibly history's first ever Pyrrhic defeat.

After plowing Natty's driveway, I got out and shoveled near her garage door and the walkway to her porch where she kept firewood in the winter. Then I returned the truck to the pole barn, fed the horses and hand-shoveled around my mailbox. If the area around the box wasn't clear, you got a pre-printed scoldy Post-it Note from the post office. The sun was just coming out as I shoveled the two walkways in front of our house and the apron near the garage door. The snow was getting heavier as it warmed slightly, and I was sweating in my coveralls. I shoveled a path to the chicken coop, brought feed for the hens, busted the ice in the two dog dishes the hens drink from, and topped them off with a bucket of fresh water from the spigot.

When I got back in, I said, "It's really regular over everything, the snow."

Molly said, "Joyce?" She was the one with a facility for literature, Kesha was more my speed. The sun was fully up now, the landscape lunar and shimmery.

Molly said, "It's pretty out there."

That was correct—and she had captured it without any struggle or pretense. That's why she has two Pushcart Prizes *and* a Best American.

Next to the fire I took off my coveralls and boots and hat and hung them all on the drying rack. Because I was going to shower, I got completely undressed. Ben was asleep and Madeleine was at work and I thought it would be funny if Molly saw me standing there naked. With my back to her I waited for a comment, but instead her phone clicked. She had taken a picture.

I said, "You need to delete that."

She looked at the picture and made a wolf whistle.

I didn't at all care about the nude picture, I was fine with it existing, my face wasn't in it anyway, but I was worried about our shared family iCloud account. "I don't want the kids to see it. Could be traumatizing."

Molly did delete the photo, but while I showered I wondered what it looked like. I knew it would not be good, but I thought maybe I might look okay in places, like my calves and leg muscles maybe because of all the bicycling; or maybe it would be apparent I had lost a little weight at some point during the past decade.

But that was not the case. After drying off, I took Molly's phone and looked at her deleted photos. I was a small, hairy blob with rolls of fat and a saggy, hair-covered ass. Completely unredeemable. All my self-deprecating patter had not prepared me for how bad I looked.

I had the urge to apologize, but before I said anything, Molly told me Jakob had texted my phone. Jakob was one of Molly's cousins who helped out on the farm. He needed help bringing round bales to the cattle. When my father in-law died, Hank had taken over the farming, but he was also Road Commissioner for the township where he lived and was plowing roads south of Scoldin. I suited back up in my damp coveralls and boots and met Jakob in the barnyard where he already had the John Deere out of the pole barn. I used the handrail and climbed the steps up the side of the tractor. Jakob held the door of the cab open and I got in the buddy seat, a plastic stool on hinges which folds down like a murphy bed.

There is a feeling of majesty being up in the cab of a tractor, cruising over the swells of the snowy landscape like a giant green ocean liner. But that's from the captain's chair. If you're hunched into the buddy seat, it can be slightly mortifying. The seat was probably meant for a child, the farmer's son, his buddy; it isn't quite large enough for a grown man, and I had to press against the glass of the cab to give Jakob enough room to maneuver the gears and levers. The buddy seat is also several inches lower then the captain's chair. Anyone looking at us would have no trouble recognizing who was superior and who was supplicant.

Jakob had made himself indispensable on the farm when Molly's dad got sick. His face had a rugged, Scandinavian handsomeness and he was good at things. I admired Jakob, but I was also jealous of his facility with the farm machines and often referred to him as "Jak-off" behind his back, because it made my nephews laugh and also because I am petty. As Jakob steered, the cab swayed and rocked gently as if we really were on a cruise ship. Under a steel shelter behind the barn was a trailer holding three round hay bales, each the size of a mini-van. Jakob turned our ship and backed up to the trailer.

Here was my first moment to be useful. I climbed down the side of the tractor with Jakob's pocket knife, which I had trouble opening and feared for one terrifying second I was going to have to climb back up and ask how, until I managed to unfold the handle and lock the blade in place. After slicing open the lightweight scrims which protect the bales, I stepped aside so Jakob could back up to the trailer hitch. These are giant machines, not easy to finesse, but Jakob was able to maneuver the 12 ton machine a few millimeters back and forth, allowing me to slip the clevis pin—about as thick as a roll of dimes—into the hitch.

When I got back in the cab I had to ask how to close the knife but Jakob just shut it himself and slipped it back in his coveralls. We had to cross a half mile of snow covered pastures to get to the herd. From the buddy seat I could see a car on Town Hall road. The township had finished plowing and Madeleine would have no trouble driving back. We rode in slow silence, with Jakob working the gears and me occasionally glancing at him from the buddy seat. He was always whistling something between his tongue and upper teeth, and today it was "It's Beginning to Look a Lot like Christmas," which I thought was odd for the first weekend of February. I couldn't wait to make fun of him with Noel and Ben. But maybe Jakob too had been thinking about the snow, trying to find some way to express the way it made him feel. I sometimes didn't give Jakob credit for much: he had started his father's eulogy with a dictionary definition of "investment accountancy," but my enmity was one sided. In fact, Jakob was affable and generous with his time. Whenever we needed assistance fixing the coop or splitting firewood, he was eager to help. And he had even come up with a better snow analogy than I had; it really was beginning to look a lot like Christmas, at least a little.

Jakob stopped at the pasture below Natty's and I hopped down to perform my second function: opening the gates so he could drive the tractor through. The drifts in the gully were so high I was almost entirely swallowed. The more I struggled to move, the more I sank as if in movie quicksand; plus I was aware of Jakob watching from high up in the warm tractor, like an amused god. By half-rolling, half-crawling, I got out of the ditch and was able to make enough room for the tractor by stomping down the snow like Cap and Almanzo, until I had enough room to swing the gates open. I walked behind as Jakob chugged tank-like to where the empty hay trailer waited to be switched out. We left the gate open but the cows weren't going to notice, they would be fixated on the new hay. The herd had sheltered the storm in the timber, but some scouts had begun emerging as soon as they heard the tractor, and now as I unhitched the trailer, a dark wave of snuffling tonnage and empty stomachs began rolling our way. By the time I had the trailer's shoe dropped securely in the snow, some cows were already working the hay, noisily pulling clumps with their teeth while more and more of the herd pushed forward.

Once the tractor was back out on the road, I stomped down more snow and closed the gate, replaced the chain, and clambered back into the buddy seat. Jakob drove us back to the barnyard. He really could have done the whole thing himself, but then he would have had to get out of the heated cab from time to time. Being cold on a snowy day? That's what you have your buddy for.

Took a nap and dreamt I was in a new city, wild and disorganized, in a bike shop but not picking out a bike, I was sweeping and dusting. BJ Anderson was in the dream and so were Stu and his dad and weirdly so was Finnegan Lee. When I woke up I thought it was strange to have Finn appearing in a bike dream. The last time I hung out with Finn was when I bought him a beer at Oasis because he had walked my reading glasses across campus after I dropped them in his office. He had asked who was my "go to porn star." I said, "I don't know. Maybe Mink Foxx," whom he then Googled and declared was "not hot." It felt like a mean thing to do.

Madeleine's door was closed so she had gotten home. Ben and Noel were stirring something on the stove. They were hunched over one of the burners, working intently. Apparently they had taken their weed grinders and cleaned the screens and blades with milk, which they were now keeping at a low, rolling boil.

I asked, "Why milk?"

Ben said, "THC needs an emulsifier and we're going to drink it."

I was always impressed with the rigor and earnestness with which Ben and Noel approached being stoned. It really was society's loss that one couldn't get high while curing cancer. The boys had purchased a squeeze bottle of Strawberry Quik to get the concoction down, and though it was going to take hours, the kitchen was already starting to smell like something between a swamp and a frat house. I went out to do some maintenance shoveling because it was spit-snowing again.

The family had talked about going somewhere for dinner but it was coming down more steadily—school had already been cancelled for Monday—so we heated frozen pizzas and again toasted the end of the Summer of Noel, which had begun when he graduated college and moved into Natty's basement, and was now coming to a close after a mere 21 months.

Much later, when Molly went to bed, I thought about going back and making a move, (politely asking for sex) but in a full house it seemed unlikely, and in light of what I had learned about my body, I thought it also might be kind to just give Molly a break, possibly permanently.

Madeleine laughed in her bedroom, I could hear her voice in delighted animation on Facetime with her friends. I went into the deBasement where Ben and Noel were watching TV sprawled across the sectional. Ben's eyes were wide and watery. I had never seen them this high before.

I told Noel, "Sleep here tonight."

"Oh-kay."

"Do not drive him home," I told Ben.

Ben said he wouldn't but I went up and took all the car keys off the wall hook anyway, and hid them in a drawer. Sophie gave me a little woof. Sometimes when we're all home and there is no structure, we forget that second walk. I put on a hoodie and stepped into my boots and took her out.

Snow fell steadily, visible only in the weak light of the lamppost where I was standing. Sophie trotted out about ten paces, squatted and peed. When she was done, she didn't come back. She put her nose up and sniffed. After awhile she turned her head and sniffed in a new direction. Her description of snow would be all bouquet and fragrance. I inhaled deeply and tried to think of the snow as she did but only came up with a mild burn in my throat.

The stars were invisible through the haze as the snow fell regular around us, on all the Libmans and on Natty and Noel, on the township trustees and the road commissioners, on Hank and Jakob and all the cattle, covering the pastures and the timber and all the folded hills where we had scattered the ashes of Abe McNair.

Sophie turned her whole body, hunched rabbinically, and pooped.

The snow is beautiful and the stars are beautiful and you want to have a poetic thought, but you're not up to it, and maybe it's not your fault. You'd like to have sex, but you're grotesque, but maybe that's not your fault either. But you can read James Joyce and you can watch Mink Foxx. And even if you can't describe the snow, you can plow it and shovel it, and you can make sure your kids get to work and don't drive in it high. There will be more snow tomorrow and maybe the only thing left in your power is to know what you can do and what you can't, and to find a way to accept that.

Sophie exhaled grandly then ambled past me toward the house. I opened the door and followed her inside.

Best Buy

Tried to buy tickets to Houston to say a final goodbye to my father, but my laptop seemed to have stopped working. Nothing happened when I checked e-mail: no hum of life, no light, just my dull face reflected on a dead screen. I loved that laptop. It was eight years old and the browser was too old to access time-wasting websites and the hardware was too out of date to take a new browser. Based on its obsolescence and my lack of self control, it was the perfect machine for me.

Went to Best Buy. Guy behind the counter asked if I had made an appointment but he went ahead and looked at the laptop anyway. He flipped it over like he was checking its diaper. His nametag said "Jimbo." After a good frown, Jimbo declared the computer dead. All he could do was migrate the data for 400 dollars.

I said, "The pictures too, or just the word files?" 'Data' didn't seem like the right word for family photos.

Jimbo said, "All of it." He said it would cost another hundred for an external drive unless I wanted to rent space on a cloud.

There was a very specific thrill at the thought of just being rid of it all. It was true there were *some* family photos in the hard drive I should save, but mostly I resented paying money to get back my writing: work that no one wanted to publish and no one would ever read. I zipped my laptop back into the case and told Jimbo I would think about it.

I could just write in my travel notebook, I thought. Part of my resistance to spending money on a new laptop had to do with the cost of round trip airfare to Texas, to the Anderson Cancer Center where my father was ending his days.

My dad had leukemia; a rare, super aggressive form, and Moira, my father's current wife, had e-mailed us, his first set of kids, to come say goodbye. The kids in my dad's new family, the one where he is the step-father, adored him. They thought he was genuinely witty, having not spent their childhoods hearing his puns and canned jokes. They weren't Jews and so didn't even know the borscht-belt comedians he stole from. Most of our contact with my dad and his new family had been through a group text thread where his health was updated regularly, answered by a series of good wishes. *Thinking of you,* my sister Emi would text. *Sending healing vibes,* my brother's wife would follow. In our family, none of us were religious and didn't want to betray even a shred of spirituality, so we were stuck with inanities that made us sound like bigger ninnies than a simple, "praying for you," would have.

My brother Mac was a doctor and he would text on a separate thread intended just for us, my erstwhile family of origin, laying out worse-case scenarios. Moira would text, *Blasts are up, so we're very hopeful!* My brother would text on the other thread: *Increased blast count is actually discouraging.* My dad's wife thought anything a doctor told her without frowning was good news. She and her kids were always upbeat and optimistic, but that was not how we were raised. Moira had played stand-up bass in the amateur folk band my father joined when he and my mom moved to the southwest. My mother would never say so, but it was obvious my father had been cheating with Moira for awhile before my mom called him on it. Moira also had a marriage to dissolve in order to marry my father, who was her third husband. At the wedding, the officiant called their marriage, "a perfect love story," and it might have seemed like that if you didn't know any of the details.

One of the other members of the folk band—all of whom were more loyal to my father than we were— picked my brother and me up at the airport since we arrived at almost the same time from different parts of the country.

"Do you think you're here to say goodbye to your father?" Travis asked once we got in his car. He was entirely bald except for a chunk of gray hair on the back of his head, which I could see from the backseat through the headrest. In the band he scratched a washboard and blew into a jug; it was that kind of band. There was a silence one might have deemed "uncomfortable" if one had been under the impression any of this was not going to suck. Mac was the one in the front seat so I let him answer.

"I suppose so," he said, finally. "Unfortunately."

"Well I don't know about that," Travis corrected. "Your father has nine lives. He's been up and down many times and I wouldn't count him out just yet."

Our dad had been in a car accident and beat colon cancer when we were teenagers so he did have at least a couple lives; nine was probably pushing it. Moira was actually the one who had said we should come and "make closure."

"Your father is doing well, at the moment," Travis said. "His blasts are up."

My phone buzzed with a text from Mac in the front seat. "Does he know I'm a doctor?"

I typed back, "He might be slow?"

Mac didn't react. Travis asked what it was like to

grow up with our father. There was an even longer pause until Mac craned his neck to look at me. "You want to field that one?"

I said, "It was okay."

Travis said, "I bet there was a lot of laughter."

I said, "As long as he didn't come home from work and find a coat hanging on the doorknob instead of in the closet."

I assumed Travis was trying to protect his own feelings, but Mac later told me he thought Travis was trying to keep *us* from being too much of a downer in the hospital room. I thought Mac was giving Travis credit for a lot of abstract thinking, though it is true the folk band spent a lot of energy keeping our father cheered up. Moira had a text thread called "Jokes N' Hope to Cope," and everyone was supposed to text funny things my father had said over the years. I blocked the notifications. It always surprised me when people—fully realized adults who had traveled or read a book—said they thought my father was funny. He had a stable of puns and corny one-liners, but if you spent more than a day with him you pretty much heard it all, especially if you said you liked Chinese food or mentioned Poland. Most of his material had not aged well and you might think it would be difficult to find a cohort who could stand his schtick, but then you might not have ever met an amateur folk musician. In the latest health update e-mail from Moira, she had described Travis as my father's "oldest and dearest friend," which confused everyone who had known my dad prior to two years ago.

The folk group my dad and Moira were in with Travis was called Sings With Strings. They played the same dozen songs over and over, and each song seemed to have a different set of verses than the ones we sang in kindergarten and were ten times longer. I once joked that the folk group was "one charismatic person shy of being a cult," but no one laughed, not even my mother who was generally receptive to a good jab at the folk band. I wondered if it was because my joke wasn't clear, that maybe I should have said, "The folk musicians would be a cult of personality if any of them had a personality." That would have been wordier and used "personality" twice, but maybe easier to understand? Either way, it was a better joke than saying you have a dental appointment at "tooth-hurty," which was one of my father's classic zingers.

The logo for the "Anderson Cancer Center" was its name with a line through the word "Cancer," presumably to suggest that they are going to eradicate the disease, although at first I thought it meant they had changed the name to Anderson Center.

If Travis really had wanted to prepare Mac and me, he might have said something about our dad's physical appearance. His face was purple and red and he could not have weighed more than 90 pounds. He looked like a bruise with eyes. In real life he had been a stocky guy, and had played hockey in a neighborhood league until he and my mother moved west, and he joined the folk band.

"How ya doin', dad?" either Mac or I asked. We had pretty much the same voice and I had trouble telling us apart.

"Still fighting." He raised a fist which had an IV tube taped along his arm. "Fighting" was the basic state of being at Anderson, where everything is geared to beating the disease, "winning," though it didn't seem like anyone ever did. We were the first of the Former Family to arrive, Mac and me, and as soon as we did Moira went off with Travis and Travis' wife, whose name I never did catch, but who was also in the band, playing something called a "hammered dulcimer."

Moira probably thought she was being kind, giving us some time with the old man, but I had found her to be a nice buffer. She made an effort at conversation, at being genial, which the rest of us really didn't. We sat for a long time in the room, me in my phone, Mac in his, and my father fighting cancer while scrolling on his phone. I was anxious just sitting there. It felt like I should be doing something. I said, "Hey dad, remember right before I went to college and you showed up at the gas station when I was working and gave me a hundred bucks?"

That's not a nice memory exactly, but it was something I occasionally thought about, that when I left home he was upset, so there was at least a day or two when he was interested in me, not knowing that I was going to return in six weeks and end up staying for years.

Mac said, "Remember when you took us to Yellowstone and we were near the crowd at the geyser and you made us say, 'Yay Yellowstone' to cover the sound of you farting?"

That one he did remember and we three chuckled.

Mac said, "Remember when you chased Barry Ziff down the block when he ding-dong-ditched our house?"

And I said, "Remember you busted the knobs off the car radio because I was playing it too loud?"

And I reminded him how he had given our dog away and Mac reminded him he had done it with the cat too and I came up with something else and Mac came up with another thing, and we were all three nodding and chuckling.

I went to the bathroom, and when I returned, my

brother and father were in the room just two of them, both on their phones, not talking to each other. They both seemed relaxed, content, normal. All the struggling and awkwardness had left the room when I did.

Near dinner, Emi and her three year old son Ornette arrived from New Mexico. A nurse was running "screens" on my father so Moira, Travis, and Hammered Dulcimer joined Mac, Emi and me in a waiting room. Two of Moira's sons were there for support. They looked to be in their twenties but I had never really talked to them. Being in that confined space with my entire family of origin, *and* my dad's new family was making me squirrely. The waiting room had a little kitchenette with a sink and fridge but there didn't seem to be any beer among the discarded sodas and pretzel bags people had left behind. I had drunk a beer and a bloody Mary in the airport but that was 10 hours ago, and then another beer and a screwdriver on the plane, but that was four hours ago, and my equanimity was starting to slip.

Moira was on the phone getting pizzas for us, but I could tell she was botching the order. She was going for 'everyone getting what they want.' In my real family, the one where I am the dad, pizza issues were solved by going big, getting twice as much as needed and eating leftovers for the next couple of days. And our pizzas were normal—pepperoni, sausage, mushroom—pizzas you could pick out of a lineup. Moira was splitting pies into halves, varying crusts and sauces. Hammered Dulcimer was pescatarian and Ornette was lactose intolerant, and Moira kept asking *everyone* if they were okay with the order.

Moira said into her phone, "Half vegetable, vegan cheese please. Yes on pineapple but red onion on only a quarter?"

And just to make matters slightly more complicated, she and Hammered Dulcimer were holding two menus from the two different, nearby pizza places: Kitchen Italia and Crusty Pie. Moira was almost done ordering when Hammered Dulcimer realized Moira was speaking with one pizzeria, but using the other menu.

"This isn't Crusty Pie?" she laughed into her phone.

This struck me as a dilemma easily remedied, or rather not even a dilemma since every pizza joint on the planet uses the exact same ingredients. When you move to a new neighborhood you don't need to go to the local parlor and ask, *do you make something called 'a veggie?'* My proof was that Moira was very nearly done and Kitchen Italia hadn't said, "Sausage? The fuck you mean?" But Moira's solution was to hang up and call the other place and start over.

I had to step away, over to my sister, where I intended to say something belittling and satisfying, but I never got it out. Emi had taken a small toothbrush from her purse. After wetting the bristles in the sink and squeezing paste on it, she took the brush and began gently rubbing Ornette's teeth. He never took his eyes off the iPad he was using, he just opened his mouth and turned his head slightly. "Spit," Emi said, and Ornette gobbed into her open palm.

I was watching Emi at the sink washing the spit out of her hand, when Travis, noticing the expression on my face, put his hand on my shoulder. He said "We're going to win this fight. You have to be strong." It took me a second to realize what Travis was talking about.

Before bed I went down to the bar in the lobby. The hotel itself is part of the Cancer Center, and the lounge is what Hemingway might have described as a sanitized and shockingly brightly lighted place. The bartender was wiping down the bar with Clorox and an empty omelet station had been rolled next to a table, ready for the morning when a chef with a white hat would make breakfast to order for visitors and residents. I had seen a photo of it in the lobby. I couldn't stand the thought of spending another minute in this hotel—this hospital—

this oncological version of *Logan's Run*, where everyone is *forced* to live past 33, and you have cancer.

I asked the bartender, "Where is the nearest bar not in this hospital?"

She made an exaggerated face. "Four miles? Ish. And the shuttle doesn't run at night." She asked if I had a car.

I liked her in the way that I tend to like everyone who will pour me a beer, so I just ordered an eight dollar Shiner Bock and caught up in my pocket notebook.

During the second beer, I told the bartender, "It says, Anderson Cancer Center, erasing cancer, but cancer has a line through it, which isn't erasing. That's crossing out. The tagline should be, 'Crossing out cancer.' Or they could just blot it out. Like 'Anderson Redacted Center.'"

She did not laugh. She said, "They have a suggestion box by the elevators." She thought they might consider it.

I said, "How's this? Anderson Cancer Center: You want 18 more months? We can give you 18 months, but it's going to be expensive. Anderson Cancer Center: Treatment hurts, but Buddha says suffering is the root of all experience."

The only other patron was several stools down. One side of his head had been shaved and light blue stitching was visible from his ear to his chin. It looked like he was drinking soda water with some limes in it. I whispered, "What's on that guy's hand?"

"Port," she said at regular volume. "It's where the injection goes when he gets his infusion. At some point, they just put it in you permanently."

I had set my alarm because my flight was super early. I walked across the street in the dark, it was not quite 4:30am, and I followed the corridors and elevators to my dad's room. No one was around and I cracked open the door.

The lights were off and he was in the bed and I thought for a moment I could see the wide expanse of the city through the window, the twinkling lights of Houston at night, but then I realized the curtains were closed. It was the machines in his room, winking at one another in the dark.

I put my hand on his shoulder and woke him. "Dad, I have to go back now."

He said, "Okay."

I said, "I love you."

He said, "I love you, too."

And I thought: I said it. My conscience is clear. I would be very surprised if those weren't his exact thoughts too. As I closed the door I could see him stir a bit, finding a comfortable spot under the covers so he could go back to sleep. He was on a lot of narcotics and they were making him itchy and I watched him scratching, trying to get comfortable. I felt bad that I had woken him needlessly, a final gift from an ungrateful son.

I can't pretend it didn't have *anything* to do with my dad, but the idea of losing any data on my computer didn't feel right, so I drove the laptop back to Best Buy. I stood in line and waited my turn. Maybe there was some photos of my dad with the kids on the hard drive which Ben or Madeleine might want to see someday. When I slid my dead laptop across the counter to a Geek Squad member named "Zach," he fiddled for a second then turned the laptop around so I could see the screen. It was booting up.

I said, "Oh my god." It was alive. "Oh my god."

Zach said, "Did the last guy pull the battery?"

"Jimbo? No he did not."

Zach said, "You'd be surprised at what pulling the battery can do."

"Oh my god."

I took out my wallet but Zach said, "No charge."

It felt like I being given an entire life back, a weird second chance to copy my files and fix things. I kept the laptop open and running while I carried it out of Best Buy. I held it out in front of me like a waiter with an overloaded tray. Other customers even stepped aside for me and one woman offered to open my car door. In the passenger seat I buckled the computer like it was a baby, like an apple shaped heart that I couldn't risk losing.

PROMPT & PRODUCT

Up at 3:15am. Wanted to keep the dream so got the handheld Tascam recorder from my desk and mumbled everything I could remember while peeing: There was a snowstorm and two teenage boys walked into our house. Dream me never used the front door in this house, which wasn't my real house, but an elongated version of the barnyard farmhouse. In real life Molly's parents had rented the house to some young folks, children of other farmers, neighbors, and they let other friends move in, townies, who trashed the house beyond habitability to the point Molly's dad had to raze the structure with a bulldozer. In the dream, the farmhouse still existed and we were living in it, and these kids barged in bringing a bunch of snow into the foyer. Both were carrying bags of mixed nuts they were selling for a high school fundraiser. I was mad but I bought some nuts while scolding them because I was also hungry. A crowd had formed in front of the house and a woman came running up and said Trent was the first great grandson of Mica Slabstone who could read. I knew it didn't matter, but really Ben had read before Trent, though Ben was younger. I was saying to the woman, *Everyone goes at their own pace. Ben was ahead of Trent but then Ben dropped out of college and*

stalled out, while Trent is graduating with a great job. He
seems super smart and capable, but when they were little,
Trent was like a retard and Ben read first.

Had coffee, egg, toast with Molly. Ben set up in the basement to work out. I listened to the Tascam recorder. Last night when I had been speaking the dream, I thought I was providing enough details to remind me of the whole thing, but when I sat down to transcribe I had forgotten almost all of it. I didn't remember who the kids were or the woman talking about Trent and Ben, even though I had the sense I knew them really well, unless that feeling was part of a lingering dream-sense. While listening to the recording, the sounds of pee and then me pouring dry cat food into the bowl are evident in the background, my voice is heavy and sleepy and I'm smacking my lips a lot and speaking through yawns. It's gross. I can hear myself hesitate before saying, "retard." I wish I had said, "Trent had less academic success," or something more acceptable, but the truth is, I've dreamt worse. The night before I dreamt Molly had a retractable vagina that dangled between her legs like a horse penis. I held it in my hand and then put it in my mouth. I probably dreamt about Trent because I saw on Facebook that he was graduating, or maybe that was part of the dream. Not sure where the horse penis came from, which, now that I think about it, was really just me having a dream about blowing a horse.

While I was transcribing, Molly vacuumed Madeleine's room so she could do yoga in it, then told me I had to use headphones because the music I was listening to would distract her. This was just the affront I was hoping for. I had only the morning to write and now Molly had spoiled my mood. Once I heard her yoga program going, I moved to the bathroom and watched a brief documentary about a woman humping her pillow on Pornhub. Some of it I watched twice. Showered. Cleaned kitchen as an act of penance. Had to empty dishwasher before loading next round. Weighed self: 175. Drove to post office to send calendar to Juli. Stopped at Hunt Club to buy ten coozies for 20 dollars as "You're Welcoming" gift for the Sitze's party. Back in car I got excited when I saw the Zubers walking out of the Ace; waved and tooted horn but couldn't gauge response from rearview mirror. When it seemed like I had safely run out of writing time, I came home and proceeded to also talk self out of exercising and into eating two quesadillas and then for some reason two bowls of granola. Since I hadn't jerked off in a week before today and the internet just got unthrottled, decided to do it again. Went Incognito. Typed "pillow" and Google guessed my next word would be "humping."

Or was it my iPad guessing? Despite the discomfort of having the machines knowing the horrors of my heart, I valiantly pressed ahead. Showered again. Weighed self: 176. Amazed to have only gained one pound considering all I had eaten. Must have jizzed out most quesadilla and granola calories. Had about 90 minutes left to work on writing, which I used for napping and then feeling bad about myself.

Toni and Nick arrived. Still felt overly fed but unlike Molly, I don't mind drinking in the afternoon, so I opened a beer and took a second in my coat pocket for the walk. We took Sophie and walked the old road, stopping to pick up Natty and her dog Spanky for some reason. Hiked out to the deer stand and then to the round bales and then back home. Most of the time Nick and I were a couple paces ahead of Toni, Molly, and Natty; the dogs were out in front of us. I had taken an extra beer for Nick too. He asked me if I had written the essay which would begin, "Everyone in my school picked a side, Beatles or Rolling Stones. I chose The Who and David Bowie," which was something I had once said to him, to which he responded, "That would be a great start of an essay." Apparently he had been serious. I told Nick I had not written the essay, and he offered me a few tips on how to start. One tip was to start with the sentence about The Who and Bowie and "see where it takes you."

As the sun began to set, we four went into the the living room and I brought out peanuts, because unlike Toni and Nick, I don't mind eating in the afternoon. Toni said she was thinking of starting a literary salon. Nick said he wanted his latest essay to be short, but once he got cooking, the essay ended up as long as all his others. Molly said she was trying to repackage all her historical stories into a single collection. I went out to close the chicken coop.

They left before dinner. Dom texted that Dave Stine had gone into hospice. We had gone to visit him at Rockford Memorial just a few days ago. The hospital television had been showing prerecorded local high school Christmas choirs and every so often I caught sight of Madeleine. Molly ordered pizzas from Alfano's and took a bath. It got very dark very early. I drove to Scoldin and got the pizzas and ate the red onions out of the salad on the way home because no one else likes them anyway. Thought about one of the pillow humpers, the second one, who had painted whiskers on her face and had tied a cat-tail around her hips. A risky choice, artistically speaking, but she had managed to make it work.

Natty drove up with Spanky and Noel and I called Madeleine from her room and Ben from the deBasement.

Spanky got on the couch and starting scratching at the beggar's lice in his fur. Noel got a beer. I ate only salad since I was unlikely to jizz out any more calories. To make the after-dinner card game more fun, I insisted— as score keeper—everyone pick an "Oh Hell" moniker. I went with "Card Shark Jimmy." Molly chose "Lilly Briscoe" from literature, Noel picked "Kenny Dennis" from novelty rap, Ben used "Krombopulos Michael" from TV. Madeleine decided to use "Malo-din," which is what Luca once called her when she was babysitting. Natty, possibly unclear that the idea is to pick a name more fun than your own, chose "Jane." Jane was out in front most of the time but flattened at the end and lost to Krombopulos Michael. Natty left with Spanky but Noel remained and got high with Ben. Madeleine drank a half serving of the cheap wine out of Molly's glass. I followed the kids into the deBasement and watched two Rick and Mortys, and then went to bed, where Molly was already asleep.

Where It Took Me
for Nick

Everyone in my school took a side, Beatles or Rolling Stones. I chose The Who and David Bowie. I told my buddy Nick this one night while we were at Stanley's Cup, a genuine dive bar in a not-so-glamorous college town, built around a not-so-glamorous university. We were drinking Pabst, not our usual order, this being the era of craft beer and we being the kind of people who keep up. I smoke meat instead of grilling and try to make my own hot sauce instead of buying. I wear flannel and have a beard. Nick wears black skinny-jeans and a leather jacket and has a clean shaven, boyish face despite being fifty like me.

I had gotten to the bar first. Nick had originally suggested going to The Forge, a brewery which he de-clared, "fantastic," possibly because it was the only one in Shucking, Illinois, the not-so-glamorous college town where we worked, and possibly because Nick regular-ly described things he liked as "fantastic." I thought the Forge served bad beer and hadn't earned its hipster vibe. The showcase IPA was called "Yellow Star," which was unhoppy and vaguely anti-Semitic. Because it was Monday night, The Forge was closed, so we caravanned in our separate cars to Stanley's Cup, which was where Nick and his wife Antonia occasionally went to take pre-dinner drinks and selfies. Toni was an accomplished writer who had recently quit and begun translating an undiscovered Portuguese poet. She was still learning the language so her method involved help from a Portuguese teacher at our not-so-glamorous university. She could probably have done it with Google Translate but I'm sure the Language Department appreciated being included as she was having quite a bit of success placing the poems. Some people aren't that good at giving up.

Though I had followed, I parked first and got my beer before him. "Whatchoo drinking," he asked. I was standing; most tables were empty but I didn't want to be the one who chose.

"Pabst," I said.

"Yeah?" he asked. "Really?"

"It won a blue ribbon."

"Fantastic." He got one for himself and I followed him to a table. Nick was an essayist, writing mostly about music with a side interest in baseball, coupled with a curiosity about nostalgia itself, often using memories from adolescence as starting points. In the time I had known him I had published one unnoticed collection of stories and he had published, like, what? Ten books? Fifteen?

A hundred? He may have started a bit further from the gate, but he had lapped me several times and there really was no longer any possibility of me catching up.

Whenever I thought about it, which honestly wasn't much, I felt embarrassed *for him*, that because his gig was with this particular not-so-glamorous-university, it meant I was the other male creative writer in the department: he was stuck with me. I slightly knew the feeling of pulling away from friends. I had gotten a story in the Paris Review when I was right out of grad school, a literary journal I now have to assure my students is prestigious if it ever comes up in class. They've also never heard of the Pushcart Prize, something I won. "Not just nominated," I add.

It felt like bragging, and unkind, when I'd told my friends, most of whom were still getting stories rejected at Cream Rises Review. It never made a difference, and eventually my friends who were going to be successful got that success, and I ended up being the one never heard from again. In the following decades, my stories found welcome homes in the slush piles of swanky mid-list lit journals: Prairie Dinghy, Misery Review, The New England Journal of Short Stories. My work has sat in manila envelopes at some of the finest undergrad work spaces in land grant colleges all over the USA. Eventually I would get a note telling me where my stories had traveled, in envelopes I had addressed, stamped with postage I had purchased.

Overall, Nick had a generous spirit, and he wanted my success possibly more than I did. He wanted—deserved—a colleague and a buddy who was his equal, with whom he could discuss his book deals or problems with agents. At Stanley's Cup, Nick said David Remnick was reading his latest book and might print an excerpt in.... Neither one of us had the courage to actually say it out loud. Nick didn't want to have to be careful around me, he wanted to talk about his writing, his success. He wanted to talk about writing with someone who didn't roll his eyes at the word "voice." And he had done everything he could to move me along. When Nick got a gig writing a regular column at some alternative rag, he tried to get me to submit work, gave me old issues to read and all the proper contacts and introductions. He urged me to keep a blog about my bicycle trips and said encouraging things like, "That would make a great start to an essay," when I made innocuous remarks about British rock acts.

The next time I saw Nick, he asked how the essay was coming. We were at the farmhouse where I live with my wife. Molly teaches the second semester of the Fiction sequence, allowing the English Department to pay two instructors to teach double the course load for half the amount they pay one tenured professor. On top of that, Molly and I, as lowly instructors, also teach courses for First Year Composition: for me Developmental Rhetoric, and for Molly English as a Second Language. When I waved off the idea of writing an essay, Nick said, "Write the opening sentence and see where it takes you. Just like we tell our students."

This was news to me. Recently in class, I had been asked by an eager young man if it was true that writers "don't write their stories." He said, "Don't writers just create characters and then those characters write our stories?"

I gave him a three second neutral response and then said, "No."

The kinds of things I tell my students is that journal editors don't really want to discover new talent, they want to publish stories by writers other editors have already discovered. I tell the students the more physically attractive among them have a better chance so they should think of their "author's photo" the same way an actor treats their head shot. I tell my students, stories mailed from Brooklyn will be taken more seriously than anything postmarked "Shucking, Illinois." I don't read my student evaluations.

But I went to the library and wrote this essay because Nick suggested I do it and being Nick's friend means something to me. And where it took me was two places, two possible endings. You can choose which ending you like better. (This kind of writing is called "interactive.")

The first ending is a memory: Nick and Toni and Molly and I are in a dive bar after AWP, the conference for writing teachers. The bar was utterly charmless, on the ground floor of a parking garage on Jackson Street in Chicago, (the only place Molly and I attend AWP because instructors don't get reimbursed for travel) and we drank Buds out of a bucket of ice, which is the way the bartender took drink orders: by the bucket. That night we all four cried, each one of us had a sad story about a sibling which brought us to tears. I'm not sure why I thought this was an appropriate place to end, except that the feeling of friendship between the four of us, the whole night really, was, well, fantastic, as my friend Nick might say.

The second ending is about me as I type this exact sentence, banging on my laptop in the library. (This kind of writing is called: "meta.") This too has a touch of the fantastic, but not in the "extraordinarily good" sense, but fantastic meaning "hard to believe."

I happen to be sitting by the music section, and recently I looked up and Nick 's book was there, on a display table with the cover facing out. I only felt the tiniest bit of jealousy when I saw the handsome cover, his name on his book. Mostly I felt pleasure. I know Molly's story collection is here too, tucked away on the fiction shelves, and Toni has several books in the poetry section, wherever that might be. My book is not here; it has a stupid title and a cover which I thought was neat when it came out, but now feels sophomoric. But I'm proud to be in the club anyway, to go on afternoon walks and share students with this trio, even if I am the least successful member.

I thought of one more possible ending, so I'm going to just tack it on here. (This kind of writing is called: "narcissistic.")

I grew up in neither city nor farmland, but in suburb; an environment that manages to combine the worst elements of the other two. I never met one single person from any aspect of my life who knew anyone else from any other part. No one from work knew my parents, no one at school knew my cousins, I never saw a familiar face at the grocery store or at a movie theater beyond the friends who came to the movie with me. I wanted to spend my life in the city, but accidentally ended up in the country, where I see people I know all the time.

The bartender at Cork and Tap is in the book club my wife never attends. The roofer who worked on my garage rides a bicycle in the group that meets on Saturdays. I see pals walking out of the hardware store when I'm driving home from the post office. Because my prior life had been so devoid of these connections, the shock I feel at seeing an unexpected, familiar face leaves me buzzing with pleasure.

All this to say, being the fourth best writer in a four person writing clique isn't the worst thing in the world, especially if you're the type of person who doesn't mind an afternoon beer or an extra meal. And if you're simple enough to enjoy waving at friends whenever you bump into them, even sitting in a library is like being at a party.

Three Days in Denmark

Breakfast starts a half hour later than we think at the Wake Up Aarhus because it's Saturday. The four of us are first at the buffet with our meal tickets, making our usual sneaky lunches, stuffing meat and cheese slices into hard rolls and wrapping them in paper towels for later, at the same time lapping up our yogurts and muesli.

The trains are busy and complicated, but we push our bicycles through the platform and get to the *vagon* listed on our tickets, where we four sit on one end, our bicycles bungee-corded nearby, waterproof bags with our clothes and toiletries sand-bagged around the bikes. Two benches have been collapsed to make bike space and there is palpable resentment among the standing-in-the-aisle Danes that our bikes are taking up seats, but Simon knew not only to make purloined sandwiches at breakfast to save money, he also knew to reserve bike space ahead of time. He had spent months planning the trip, which we are doing in late spring because it is the only time his wife, Cloris, can get away from Calgary where she is a dean at the university. Molly and I have flexible schedules as instructors at an Illinois state university, not the good one.

Nearing Gråsten we gear up for the frenzy of getting

our bikes and bags off the train but the conductor push-
es her way through the aisle toward us. She is in full
uniform, yellow hair neatly tucked under a blue cap. She
informs us she is "in charge" so we have don't have to
rush. "Nothing to worry about," she guarantees the train
won't move until we have our stuff on the platform. Tap-
ping her lapel pin she repeats, "I'm in charge."

The conductor says she likes Simon and Cloris' shirts.
Both are wearing Canadian themed bike jerseys: Cloris'
has a Maple Leaf and says University of Calgary and Simon's is of a Mountie in a wide hat standing in a forest
of pines. This one she particularly likes.

Addressing me, she says, "In Danish there is a word
for the kind of fat you are," and she makes a gesture like
someone carrying an enormous baby. She can't think
of the English word so she keeps pointing to my stom-
ach. Simon, Cloris and Molly start to guess. "Fatso?"
"Beer-belly?" "Puss-gut?" "Tubby? You know, like big fat
tubby tub-gut?"

The conductor is shaking her head. She's getting frustrated. "No, no, no…" She opens her arms wide to show
how fat I am, repeats the word in Danish and it kind of
sounds like "Buddha." They're all pointing at my stom-
ach now. "Buddha-belly?" Buddha gut?' "Buddha something, right? Big fat Buddha?"

Everyone is laughing and laughing as we slide into the station. The conductor says again, "No need to rush."

Simon and I hand the bikes to Cloris and Molly, who have stacked the bags on the platform; we are rushing, it's a habit. Once the train has gone and we reattach the bags to the racks, all we can talk about is what a nice lady that conductor was. "Really nice," Molly says. Simon and Cloris agree: she was a really, really nice lady.

The toilets are broken at the station—someone has stuck a kroner in the slot where the credit cards go, it's a pay toilet, so we go across the street to a Shell station but they have no bathrooms. Simon decides we'll just "hold it" and has me lead because he's tying to save battery on his watch. I have the route on my Garmin, but the Garmin is usually a beat or two behind and I don't actually know what city we're riding to because Simon made all the plans and I'm too embarrassed to ask. I know we're on a loop and generally heading back to Copenhagen, but that's still days away. I go straight through the first intersection and by the time I realize I should have turned, even before my Garmin beeps that I'm off course, Simon has already taken a right turn and is out in front again, and that's the end of me leading.

The day is gorgeous: sunny, slight breeze, cool but manageable with a light jacket. We find ourselves pedaling in rare, hilly terrain, with a pretty descent into Sønderborg. Stopping at a historical marker, I'm stunned to see how close we are to the border. When we got off the train I had gotten a text from Verizon about cell rates in Germany; I had assumed it was some weird glitch. Part of the appeal of travel is the thrill of discovery, learning something new about yourself and about the world, and while, "Denmark borders Germany," isn't much of a revelation, it is a start.

Each of us carries two bags on our bikes. I have a third slung across my back, a firetruck-red messenger bag which I call "My *bouche*." I insist *bouche* means bag in French. I'm the only one in our quartet who doesn't speak French: Molly lived in France as an au pair, Cloris has citizenship in three countries, including one with French as an official language, and Simon is smart. Although they argued the first day—especially Cloris who would point to her face, "*Bouche mouth, bouche mouth,*" eventually I wore them down. Now at lunch even Cloris will say, "Is the lock in Dan's *bouche*?"

We pause for coffee and pastry at a Trip-Advisor vetted bakery, selected by Simon in Calgary months ago. Simon is a Geography professor and I've joked that the only reason he travels is to verify how well he did planning and researching the trip. At the grocery store across the street, I buy five Danish beers for the B&B.

Molly says, "Why not just get one or two?"

"That's why I have the *bouche*," I tell her. Part of the worldliness I hope to gain while traveling involves sampling local beers. After adjusting the strap, the five pints actually make the *bouche* a bit heavy, but I'll be damned if I'll admit it.

Simon and Cloris ride side by side in front, Molly and I about ten paces back. We originally met the Malcolms at Temple Beth-El in Rockford, Illinois. They were on a brief stop in the middle of Cloris' meteoric rise up the ranks of academia, while Molly and I had stalled on our journeys to nowhere. Back then we all worked at the same college, Simon and Cloris as professors and Molly and I instructors on renewable yearly contracts. Simon was the first person I ever saw take out his cell-phone to settle an argument; it felt like being sucker-punched. Molly and I jokingly referred to them as "The Successful Version of Us," and somewhere between Cloris' being named Dean and the BMW, it stopped being a joke.

The wind picks up as we ride past small fields of wheat waving so robustly they resemble storm tossed seas. Wild flowers and poppies grow scattered among the rye and barley. I say to Molly, "We should take a picture."

She says, "You could have brought your GoPro but you never use it."

The B&B Simon booked for us is being run by a guy from Oklahoma and his Danish wife, Trine. They show us around their house and offer us Carlsberg beers. I open my *bouche* and show them my beer. "Are these breweries near here?" I ask.

Trine has narrow glasses and a kind, round face. She says, "These beers are from Sweden."

The yard is charming and it's impressive how they live—simply, mostly off the grid, reusing and repurposing when possible. Trine bikes to work every day and she and Oklahoma sleep outside under a covered platform, even in winter. Cloris and Trine discuss the flower garden. Simon shows Oklahoma how his watch connects to the cadence sensor on the bike. Molly naps in our upstairs bedroom. I sip one of my foamy, warm Swedish beers.

Toward evening we take a short ride into town and eat at Øhav Bar, sitting on benches facing the archipelago, a small table in front of us for food and drinks. We're just settling in when my knee knocks the table, spilling Simon's gin and tonic.

"At home we all call him Dribbles," Molly says, which is not exactly true, she does, but I don't dispute it because I'm busy mopping the spill with napkins, dashing across the gritty beach to Øhav's patio to get Simon another gin and tonic. I also order a large plate of French fries and mayonnaise for everyone to share.

"My treat for spilling." I hand Simon his new gin and tonic and then nudge the fry plate, which knocks my beer bottle over.

"Dribbles!" Molly shrieks. This time I've splashed her leg and there are no more napkins. I run and get a rag.

"It's okay," I try to put on a good face after returning from the bar with a new beer. "I regretted not getting this beer in the first place. I made sure it was actually Danish," I pointed to the *"Brygget i København"* on the label. Brewed in Copenhagen.

Simon looks at the bottle, hones in on the part where it says, *"Alkohol fri."* He holds his phone up and shows me the on-screen translation: "Alcohol free."

Before bed at the B&B Molly teaches Simon and Cloris how to play Oh Hell with a deck of cards they brought. I keep score in my notebook. Cloris says it's really easy, but she doesn't mean it as an insult. On the contrary, she seems delighted to be able to master it quickly and make short work of us.

The "beds" are fine, narrow twins under a slanted doll-house roof, but the "and breakfast" is slightly awkward, though presented to us with pride and effort, at a fancy table in the living room. Trine points out the little yogurt cups are topped with edible flowers from her garden. It takes a while for Oklahoma to bring out the large pot of coffee because he doesn't drink it and doesn't seem to know how on edge everyone is until it comes out. When he leaves the pot, I get up to pour for everyone. Cloris, whose cup I begin with, says, "Why are we having Da—" and she stops talking. I assume what she hasn't said is, "—n pour the coffee despite his being incompetent and spilling so much even his own family derisively refers to him as Dribbles?"

There actually is a slight tremor in my hand but I manage to pour coffee into all four delicate cups on the little saucers without spilling. Even I'm pleasantly surprised. We say goodbye and after tossing our leftovers to the pig across the road, (we were told he waits for guests to do just that,) we bike down to the ferry, three miles, all downhill to the pier where we walk our bikes into the belly of the ship.

I lean back on a bench, and just as our journey to Ærø Island begins, all the coins spill out of my pocket and go rolling across the deck. I'm still chasing them down when the ticket guy approaches. The coins had been piling up in the saddle bag of my bike and I had hoped to unload them, but he only takes credit. After he slides my card, some of the passengers approach. They have collected the coins and bring them to me by the handful, smiling kindly.

Pockets bulging, I head inside to use the bathroom. The door is locked. I stand and wait. It's taking awhile, and then one of the other passengers opens the door and goes in. The bathroom had not been locked, I had pushed instead of pulled. Now I have to wait for him to finish and come out.

Simon walks over and I say, "It's occupied."

He says, "Is it a one seater?" He pulls open the door and looks. "Two seats but there's another guy." He goes in. I keep waiting.

For the last part of the ride I take up a spot at the rail and put on Spotify. I have not listened to any music since the trip began because we're always together and it would feel rude. But here I am alone, looking at the islands sliding by, the water churning below, it's all rather majestic, so I crank it up. I'm alone and the ship is noisy so I sing—loudly—the Robert Pollard song, *Frequent Weaver Who Burns*. I have it on repeat and I keep singing it, the same song, over and over until the ship docks and we get back on the bicycles.

The island is pretty and the roads are narrow with very little motor traffic. Molly and I are several paces behind Cloris and Simon, and I say, "You're doing great hon, you've got this."

Molly says, "Did you notice everyone move away when you started singing?"

"On the ferry? I didn't know anyone could hear me."

"One woman said you might be mentally ill. She thought maybe you panhandled by singing in the streets which explained the coins."

I thought it *had* seemed awkward for a bit when the ferry ride ended, no one quite making eye contact with me. I let Molly get ahead of me as we pedal to Ærøskøbing and stop for lunch, eating little fish sandwiches on boards. Simon shows me a picture he took with his phone: me at the rail, mouth open, *bouche* slung on my back: a fool bellowing at the top of his lungs to the sea.

This evening's B&B has a dog named Bowie, a chocolate colored lab who chases a rag-toy and drops it back at our feet. We have a living area with a kitchenette and bunk beds in the back of a ranch house. The rambling courtyard has a chicken pen and several stray cats. I sit outside and read. As I toss the toy for Bowie, I realize I have had a vague notion that people in other countries are constantly thinking about Americans. Like, a Dane might have a good day, but at bedtime he would idly wonder how much better his day would have been in America. Or he might enjoy his home, yet still be aware that something was off with it, compared to American homes.

When the sun goes down, the proprietor of the B&B delivers tomorrow's breakfast: eggs from his coop and some meats and cheeses. Simon is on his iPad trying to find shortcuts, places to trim tomorrow's route. Molly's friend Nina will be meeting us in our destination city—this has been in the offing for months—but none of us can figure how it will actually happen. Nina is a Greenlander and was Molly's roommate when she lived in France 25 years ago.

We play Oh Hell in the yard, Bowie at our feet. Cloris is drinking gin and I'm drinking another warm pint of Swedish beer from my *bouche*. While I shuffle, Simon says, "Danny is a card bender."

It's true! The cards are noticeably more bent after I shuffle them. Cloris, who has been shuffling for Molly, says, "I can shuffle for you too if you want. Or Simon can if that would be less..." And she trails off because, I assume, none of us can figure out what the end of that sentence might be.

"I'll just try harder," I say, but when it comes to my next deal, I spread the cards out on the table and swish them around like I'm finger panting, then restack. As far as travel-inspired revelations go, "Foreigners aren't always thinking about America" and "I'm a card bender," are disappointing. I'm still hoping for something more profound, life altering.

Each couple is sleeping on a bunkbed in a separate alcove. Molly takes the top bunk because I get up to pee so much. When the lights are off I say, "You were worried about riding every day but you're doing awesome. I'm proud of you."

She says, "How come you never use the GoPro? It wasn't cheap." A little while later, as I'm drifting off, she adds, "I thought it was a nice gift, but you never use it."

When I get up to pee, I have to cross in front of the alcove Simon and Cloris are bunked in and it triggers bright, automatic lights in the corridor. I'm barefoot and the acrylic floors are warm. Back in bed I worry I left the seat up. Simon has told me a number of times it bothers Cloris when I do that, although she has never said anything. I get back up to check the seat. It's down but this time I trigger the lights directly over their bunkbed and I can hear one of them muttering.

Everyone's alarm goes off at once and there is an immediate frenzy in the kitchen as we prepare the breakfast. As a chicken owner myself, cracking eggs is my métier, so I grandly take an egg in one hand and smack it against the pan, but some of it dribbles on the counter.

"Danny!" Simon shouts.

It's really just a drop or two, and I wipe it up with a paper towel and crack another egg.

"Danny!"

I dribbled again.

"If my contributions aren't being appreciated I'll just pack my own bag," I sniff and leave the kitchen. No one stops me. As penance, I eat less than everyone else and then do the dishes and load them into the washer. When I am done scrubbing the pan, Molly looks over my shoulder. She says, "Not good," and rewashes it.

On our way out, Simon picks up the pan Molly washed. "Hey, looks good, Danny."

I have a flash of actual pride, but then I remember. "Molly re-washed it after me," I tell him. She's standing right next to me anyway.

There is still excitement whenever we roll out; organizing our stuff back into bags, fastening them to the racks, Cloris and Simon synching their watches and Garmins, the first pedal-pumps of the day. At the pier, our group has ten minutes to spare before getting on our final ferry so we look in the gift shop. I spend four

Kroners for an iron bottle opener shaped like a sailor's scaffolding-knot and as we walk to the ticket booth, I show it to Simon.

"Will that actually open a bottle?"

I see his point- it is slightly misshapen. "I was just trying to get rid of coins. Lighten the load."

He tests the weight in his palm. "But isn't this much heavier than the coins?"

As we approach the ticket window, Simon says, "Two Adults and two children." His eyes widen at me. "Oops. Sorry about that. Four adults."

This ferry ride is crowded and I don't sing; Simon and Cloris don't sit anywhere near us, just in case. Molly seems glum so I ask what's wrong.

"Blood sugar."

We had saved the breakfast rolls and meat and cheese for later, and the egg was not enough fuel to get Molly to lunch. I give her a sandwich from the *bouche* and she eats it. Feeling perkier, she says, "When we get back you should give Dom your GoPro. I bet he would appreciate it. It wasn't cheap."

Once across the Baltic sea we resume pedaling in Svendborg. Even the most remote road has a bike lane or markings for cyclists. The towns themselves seem sleepy. It's summer so maybe everyone is traveling. We bike across a long, windy bridge and stop at a designated picnic area on the other side.

"I already ate mine," I say grandly when I hand Cloris her sandwich. Molly might be embarrassed to have already eaten, so here is an opportunity to be a hero and I give Molly my sandwich. When Simon comes back from pissing, Cloris says, "Dan ate without us." Simon takes his sandwich and the three of them eat. I stand and stretch in a kind of showy way. Molly might say something here, *Actually I'm the one who who ate a sandwich, he's being chivalrous, and now the poor guy has no lunch.* The Malcolms would give me credit for being a good husband *and* Molly wouldn't lose face. On the contrary, she would look selfless because she tried to make me look good: an endless reflected glory feedback loop! Plus, we would be a *good couple*, like we say about Toni and Nick because they always click the heart on each other's tweets, like we say about Mandi and Zuber because they sit with each other and talk just the two of them even at crowded parties, like we say about Cloris and Simon because they're so supportive of each other's careers. I try to convey all this to Molly via facial expression, but raising my eyebrows doesn't quite capture it, and she isn't looking anyway.

We chug along most of the afternoon. It's a fun ride,

although getting overcast and more urban. I feel a wave of gratitude toward Simon. He didn't need to invite us on this trip and I never would have thought of doing it on my own. A year ago I would have been hard pressed to find Denmark on a map. And yet, here we are. Simon calls out that we're three kilometers away from our destination.

I pedal alongside Molly. "That's about two miles," I say. "You got this! Just the distance from our house to the highway and back"

She looks over at me. "Why would you say that? That's very discouraging!"

This gives me pause. I had hoped to be *encouraging* by telling her how close we were to our destination, but it turned out my words had been *dis*-couraging, the *opposite* of the effect I wanted. Those miles do pass slowly, but I am cheery because the evening is setting up nicely for me. Molly will be hanging with Nina, and Simon and Cloris already talked about going off by themselves assuming I would be with Molly. I was going to fall through the cracks, bike out alone, sit in a bar, sample local beer. I find myself really liking the town. Nykobing Falster has a river but isn't flashy, a little run down maybe, feels like a Danish version of Rockford, Illinois.

Finding the B&B is easy and we have two of the three

rentable rooms; the other one is occupied with Germans also on a bike trip, so Nina, who drove several hours to meet us, could not rent it. We're on the second floor of a small duplex and our room has a coffee maker and a view of a small fountain. While we're changing out of our riding clothes Molly gets a text.

She says. "Nina booked a room in another hotel but they're driving over now."

They? Shit! I'm stuck, I think. Stuck. If Nina has brought her husband then I'm stuck!

When Nina arrives, Molly and I go down and meet them on the driveway. The "they" turns out to be her daughter. A child. She's small. Thirteen and seems sullen; this is who I am stuck with. Molly and Nina are going to talk old times with each other and this child and I are going to be listening.

Everyone is being polite, smiling and nodding. Nina speaks in French to Molly, introducing her daughter, Sigríður, then pivoting to English when Molly introduces me. Nina says we need to take a car instead of walking because Sigríður recently twisted her ankle. I haven't been in a car in two weeks and this feels like a punishment. I ride in the back seat next to the girl. Sigríður looks out her window and I look out mine as the two adults in front natter away. Stuck! I catch my own reflection in the window: I'm actually pouting. Nina says something to Sigríður in Danish. Sigríður picks up her phone, and changes the song as we drive over the bridge into the downtown.

"She can't even get iTunes to work without me," she says.

We park the car and walk through a narrow passage between buildings. The girl is limping, but we get to a restaurant, the only one open on a Monday. Down the street I see Simon and Cloris on bikes, they seem to be having trouble finding somewhere to eat.

We are seated and given giant menus. Nina says to Sigríður, "Tell Molly and… Tell them how you hurt your ankle." Nina says to me. "She hurt it for her father, on a hunt honoring him." Nina speaks English quickly when speaking to Molly, but slows down when talking to me. "A reindeer hunt. Do you know what a reindeer is?"

"Yes."

Sigríður puts her menu down. She says, "Sooo, I had to make it just a baby reindeer because I had to carry it by myself."

I'm startled for a moment as Sigríður speaks in perfectly inflected, colloquial English. She tells us that outside of Nuuk, Greenland where her father lived, she went on a rite of passage hunt on the anniversary of his death. Sigríður had crept around the woods at night and stalked the reindeer whom she killed with a rifle and hauled out of the woods. She's not exactly enthusiastic about telling the story, but she is polite and confident. She uses her fist to demonstrate wrapping leather straps around the belly of the baby reindeer so she could more easily drag the animal to a clearing where her family was waiting.

I am riveted by the story, almost breathless, which is when I suddenly get it—the epiphany I've been traveling for! I am not the one stuck tonight: Sigríður is. This child, fluent in four languages, competent enough to hunt wild animals *and* use the apps on her phone, is stuck entertaining an overweight, under-educated, fifty year old baby, because her mother is making her. This is the sort of revelation people climb mountains to achieve, and here I got mine sitting in an empty burger joint on a Monday night in Danish Rockford.

When the story is over I feel chastened, humbled, and I attempt to be just as interesting as she is. "I am making an informal study of local, Danish beers." I tell her, holding up my bottle. "Like this. Do you know if this town is near here?"

Sigríður says, "That's from Stockholm." And when I don't react she adds, "In Sweden. The label is in English."

Having struck out everywhere else Simon and Cloris eventually show up and we all move to a larger table. I can see they are disappointed to have ended up with us, but I ask Sigríður to repeat her hunting story, and by the time she's describing how she sliced the cavity into the reindeer's chest so she could tuck the head inside, Cloris is mesmerized.

"You can talk to Dan," Cloris says to Simon. "I'm fine with *Sigrid*."

Cloris is already using a nickname and she offers to let Sigríður stay with them if she ever travels to Canada. "If you want to study in Calgary, I'm sure I can get you funded."

Sigríður smiles. She seems happy to answer Cloris' questions about life in her boarding school, which it had not occurred to me to ask about. They have a good rapport, which makes me want to hug Cloris.

Back in the car Sigríður gives Nina directions on how to cross back over the bridge. She points out to me that her mother has *already* forgotten where their hotel is. "She relies on me for everything," Sigríður says.

"Same with Molly," I say. "On me."

Nina drops us off in front of the B&B and we wave goodbye. Molly asks them to meet us for breakfast and Nina says she will, Sigríður says she wants to sleep late so won't be coming.

As we unlock our door, Molly asks, "What did you think of Nina?"

"She was nice," I say. "Really, really nice!"

When Simon and Cloris get back the four of us play Oh Hell in the common room of the B&B, drinking from a bottle of Akvavit they bought. We all agree it tastes like rye bread, but bizarrely, everyone else thinks that's a negative. I insist this time we use card monikers. I offer "Dribbles," for my name. Simon chooses, "Nykøbing Falster Card Shark," Molly goes with her standard "Sleepy," and Cloris chooses "Dame Cloris." Throughout the game I refer to her as "Damn Cloris," as though I can't read my own writing. It's a sophomoric joke and Cloris barely notices, she patiently corrects me each time. "*Dame.* Dame Cloris." I could have stopped when no one laughed the first time, but I kept it up the whole game, which is something you can do when you're the one keeping score.

Jaycee Halper invited me to volunteer at The Greens. I would be going on bike rides Monday mornings with the clients, adults with developmental disabilities, on side by side tandems called JoyRides. Jaycee was married to Tug Halper, a local insurance salesman who was friendly and well-liked in Hoogler County. Years before, Tug had contacted me via Strava and invited me to ride with him on the single-track bike path in Lowell Park. This was in the winter and I put my fat tire bicycle next to his in the bed of his pickup truck and climbed up in the heated cab. He said, "My friend Jim Everet went on a date with your wife."

I said, "Recently?"

Tug didn't laugh. He said it was when they were in high school.

I knew Jim Everet had not ever dated Molly, but had gone to prom with her sister, Bridget. Bridget had a funny anecdote about it: Her dad, Abe McNair, had earlier that day dumped a dead cow near their driveway for a renderer who had not shown up. The cow bloated in the sun and when Jim arrived to pick up Bridget, the buzzards were swarming and pulling out the intestines. Bridget had been humiliated, although Jim Everet had gone on to become a large animal veterinarian—we used him on the farm—so it hadn't damaged him any. I once joked to Molly that Bridget's prom had been Jim Everet's first house call. She didn't laugh.

I told Jaycee I would be happy to help at The Greens. Previously I had volunteered with a non-profit filling out tax forms for people in low income housing, trying to qualify them for the Earned Income Tax Credit, under the false impression it would help me understand the tax code. Another time I advocated for children in family court, hoping it would quell my anxieties about having my own children taken from me. The JoyRides would be in that same tradition: I could do something useful *and* get to ride a bicycle.

Our house was cold that Monday in June for my first Greens JoyRide. Overcast. It also turned out our lawn was full of cows that had come over the new cattleguard Hank installed so he and the other farmhands wouldn't have to keep stepping down from their four wheelers, unchain the gate, drive forward, then stop again to close and rechain the gate. This was a tedious process that had gone on for decades even when the farmers rode horses, but within a year of Abe McNair's death, Hank and the other farmers had persuaded Natty to get the metal grates.

"Cows won't cross," Hank had assured us. "Even if you just paint lines on pavement, they won't cross."

Not sure about painted lines, but our cattle regularly crossed over the guard to graze on the greener grass of our lawn. Despite their fearsome size and resting bitch faces, cows are fairly compliant and as soon as they saw me coming they turned and easily hopped back over the cattle "guard." The cows knew they had transgressed but they never had much of a plan.

Molly was petting the dog when I got back in. She still had her flesh-colored Breathe Right Nasal Strip across her nose which gave her the not-unappealing look of having a snout. Molly was always searching for something to order her life: going on annual ten day silent meditations, giving up coffee, doing yoga, de-cluttering the house, giving up coffee again and replacing it with hot mushroom water, Ekhart Tolle, counting calories, mixing chicory in coffee to reduce caffeine, vegetarianism, Noom, waiting until lunch for coffee, and now it was breathing only through her nose. Sophie, on the other hand, had fewer interests and little inclination to change her behavior. She liked to sit on the lawn and bark at birds and beg for pita chips whenever she heard the bag rustle. In the summer, Sophie had allergies which made her paws itch after walking in the pasture; she chewed her pads so much they bled. Molly was still trying to distract Sophie via "tum rub" when I headed out.

I rode my Marrake$h bicycle six miles into town to The Greens, where Jaycee was already out front with Susanna, The Greens director. The building was low and long, like a grammar school, and Jaycee led me to the garage across the parking lot. The two of us rolled the the bikes out, making several trips until all five were in a line by the door of the main building. Each bike had two side by side seats, two butterfly handlebars, two sets of pedals and chains, but the bike was easily operated with only one person pedaling and steering. The pedals had Velcro straps and the seats had seatbelts. Behind the seats, each bike had a single mesh basket, large enough for a jug of water and some cups.

The other volunteers were arriving and Susanna assigned each one a bike and gave them a buck slip with three names on it. Susanna and I knew each other because she had been a few years ahead of Molly in school, and when we first moved to Hoogler County we attempted a friendship with her and her husband, but it didn't take. I recognized all the volunteers as local townspeople, although I didn't know any of them other than Jaycee and Susanna.

My first riding partner was an older, rail-thin woman named Edie, who wore long gloves and shrieked with joy whenever she saw someone she could wave to, regardless if it was a walker in the park or a distant car. She was sweet and lost interest in me once we started pedaling in favor of waving to everyone else.

Park West was just behind The Greens' building and Edie and I rode mid-pack since this was my first day. The route took us past the fenced-in dog area and once around the senior center, then across the wooden pedestrian bridge that went over the wild flowers Harley Heartly planted before his falling out with the Park District. At the midway point we stopped at the picnic tables for the clients to step down from the bike and get a cup of water from the jugs we carried in our baskets. The full loop took about 50 minutes including the water break.

When we returned to The Greens, Susanna walked the riders back into the building and emerged with a new set of clients, presenting them to the volunteers like debutantes at a high-society ball. My second rider was a slump-shouldered man named Dwayne.

"Dwayne's not going to pedal," Susanna told me, bending down to Velcro his feet. "Or talk."

I nodded to Dwayne, he did not respond. As we rode,

I made little attempts at conversation, pointing out a bluebird in one of the pines and saying how nice the weather was. He looked where I was indicating, but said nothing. The undulations of Scoldin's Park West, though slight, felt significant when riding alongside someone who wasn't pedaling. Or talking.

My third bike-mate was a delightful woman named Gail who didn't pedal but was very chatty. Her first question after we were introduced was, "Do you have a pet?"

Gail's sunhat had a brim so wide I had to lean away slightly as we pedaled.

"What is your dog's name?" she asked. "How old is she? Does she behave?"

I told Gail that Sophie did behave mostly but that when she was a little she used to chew up shoes and pillows. Gail turned to me, her eyes wide. "Oh boy!" she said slowly. "Oh boy, oh boy! Did you get her in trouble? Did she do it again?"

I tried to assure Gail that Sophie wasn't in trouble, that all this had happened a long time ago, but she seemed genuinely worried that I was upset at the dog. When I pointed out the pretty wildflowers to change the subject, Gail would go back to it.

She said, "Does your dog chew anything else?"

"No, no. She's a good dog. That was just puppy behavior. We never got mad at her and she grew out of it."

Gail shook her head, not quite sure if she believed me. "Oh boy."

After the first ride I had been nearly teary from my own magnanimity, but as I finished the last one I was mostly worried about the germs on the handlebars and seatbelts and went in to the building to scrub my hands. Molly and I would be traveling overseas with another couple later in the summer, and the idea that I might get sick and miss the trip made me nervous.

On the way home I saw Zuber jogging and I asked how his weekend was. He said it had been "contemplative," but that he had gained weight. I didn't know if he gained the weight over the weekend or just in general, and I had ridden past too quickly to clarify.

I started the second JoyRide Monday by opening the chicken coop and collecting seven eggs, none pecked. Soft boiled two and noticed Copenhagen Bicycles had emailed overnight answering that I could use my own pedals when we rented our bikes, as long as I dropped them off before we left on Sunday. This didn't sound right, and when I checked the schedule, Simon had us starting the bike trip Saturday. Two weeks of B&B reservations were contingent on us getting the bikes one day earlier.

I nervously texted Simon about the discrepancy. I had previously gone on one great trip in my life, to Asia, and it was because Simon had planned it and let Molly and me come along. Now he had taken a notion to ride bikes through Denmark. He had planned the route, researched the accommodations, asked me only to handle the bike rental, and now it seemed like I had screwed it up.

At The Greens, I was engaging the kickstand on the Marrake$h when I noticed there was already a large crowd of volunteers. Tug Halper ambled up to me.

"Susanna didn't know you were coming."

I said, "I thought it was every Monday."

I was thrilled to suddenly have my morning back, but Tug said, "This is perfect because I actually have some work to do,"

"I have work to do too," I lied. Suddenly getting my Monday back was very exciting. "You stay, I'll come next week."

He said, "No, no." Tug had a bland, featureless face, which always put me in the mind of Arendt's observation regarding the banality of evil. He reached for his car keys. "There's a bunch of pretty ladies for you to ride with." He gestured to the volunteers as though I could have my pick.

"I really don't mind leaving," I was saying, but Tug had clearly won, possibly because closing his car door was more definitive than anything I could manage with my bicycle.

I stood quietly with the volunteers as Susanna came out of the building. She looked up from the buck slips and said, "Where's Tug?"

Jaycee said, "He left."

I said, "I thought I was supposed to come every Monday."

Susanna squinted at her buck slips. "We can just make some changes," and she looked over at Jaycee. "Some *surprise* changes." She used the same tone when the residents said they didn't need to use the seatbelt. She handed me the buck slip with Tug's name on it.

The pretty ladies turned out to be the two blonde women who always dress identically, same jean jackets and boots, same frosted hair and polished nails. I often saw them huddled over the bar at Cork and Tap looking like they wanted to be asked why they were dressed in twin-sister Halloween costumes, just so they could glare at you and not answer. Tug had been talking to them when I rode up and they had been laughing. Now they were not laughing.

I got my first rider, a small man named Gino who

said, "Shall we start," like he was doing me a favor. He thanked me for coming and buckled his own belt. I was mid-pack again, and as we headed out toward the Senior Center, one of the back wheels started wobbling on the bike in front of me. The bike shuddered and listed to one side. I hopped out to fix it. I thought the quick-release had just popped open, but once we all started riding again, the wheel loosened and fell off. Both riders had to get off the bike so I could turn it over and rethread the entire skewer.

When we were moving again, I said, "Great day," to Gino. Everyone had been disappointed I was here instead of Tug, but I had fixed something on the bike that no one else was able to, so it was a good thing I had stayed. It only took me another second to remember Tug was also a cyclist—that's how he found me on Strava. Not only would he have fixed the wheel, he would have gotten it right the first time.

When we got back, Susanna was already being told about the wheel by one of the twins. I jumped in and said, "The wheel came loose," which was information she already had. I wanted someone to say, *This guy fixed it just as good as Tug*, but no one did.

For my next ride I got Gail again and we again talked about Sophie, what sort of weekend she (Sophie) had and where she (Sophie) stayed in the house when I mowed the lawn. She (Gail) could actually hold a conversation, albeit a narrowly focused one, and I genuinely liked her company.

Before the third ride, Susanna walked out with a client on her arm. He carried himself like an elderly person, walking carefully, one foot in front of the other; although his face was wide and youthful looking. He was smiling as Susanna walked him to the group.

He said, "Where's Tug?"

"Tug's not here today," Susanna said.

His face fell. He looked around randomly for someone to engage with, and standing close to me he said, "I was looking forward to speaking with Tug Halpern."

I didn't feel like I could look him in the eyes, although his eyes weren't tracking together so I couldn't have anyway. He was seated on one of the twin's bikes and as Susanna velcroed his feet to the pedal, he said. "I wanted to get Tug's opinion about a sign for the rose bush."

My buck slip said I would be riding No Talk No Pedal Dwayne. As Dwane sat and I pedaled along, I wondered if the fact that he didn't talk meant that he didn't enjoy being talked to or if he thought it was rude that no one talked to him. The only analogy I could think of was being talked to by a dentist during a cleaning. I decided

I would speak to my comfort level, not his, and when I felt like saying something I would, but not force it. I said a few things to Dwayne, like "speed bump" and "Wind's at our back now."

I was enjoying the effort it took to pedal the JoyRide alone when the bike in front stopped. I rolled up alongside and said, "You guys okay?" It was the twin with the guy who wanted to speak with Tug Halpern.

The twin said, "He said he wanted to stop." The four of us were quiet a moment, none of us sure what was happening. So I directly asked him, "Are you okay?"

He said, "My strap keeps getting tighter." With his wide face he looked like a distressed Humpty Dumpty. I got off my bike and checked where Susanna had strapped his feet to the pedal. She had looped one of his shoelaces weirdly around the crank and it must have been tightening on every stroke. I had trouble undoing the knot, but when I did he gave a big relieved sigh.

After the water stop, where Jaycee and the twins grouped off and didn't talk to me, I was out front and pedaled as fast as I could. The winds were at our backs and I said to Dwayne, "This is great, isn't it?"

Dwayne grinned and nodded once. No Talk No Pedal Dwayne had responded. It was only for a second and it might just have been a bump in the road jostling him, but I was glad that that I stayed. I pedaled fast and Dwayne and I got back to The Greens several minutes before the rest of them.

After I put the JoyRides back in the garage I checked my phone. Simon Malcolm said he would take care of the issue in Denmark. He had texted: "Whatever happens it won't be as bad as the boat ride in Phuket."

On that other trip, we had boarded an especially unseaworthy vessel in Thailand. The boat had no life preservers and shook violently as the captain sped across the Andaman Sea. My joke at the time was that if we capsized, the headline of the university newspaper where we all worked would have read:

Dean Cloris Malcolm, Professor Simon Malcolm
& 2 Instructors Lost at Sea

This was probably my best joke ever, but one had to work at DeKalb State University to know the incessant, pointless humiliations regularly heaped on instructors to get it. Simon and Cloris did work at DSU at the time and got the joke, but they had not laughed.

On the next Monday, Madeleine needed an early dismissal for her ear appointment with Dr. Furg. I asked Molly if she would make the call.

"I do it all the time," I reminded her. "But I have to get out to The Greens."

She said, "I have to meet a yoga instructor at the studio before class."

I didn't answer. We both had plenty of time, but neither one of us liked calling the school for an early dismissal because the secretary was scoldy and suspicious. She never said anything, but you could tell she didn't approve. As Molly left she yelled, "Fine! Text me the number."

The number was in her phone, just as it was in mine, in our shared contacts, so I called the school and took care of it, as we both had known I would. I was feeling bad about my total cave when Molly texted, "I fed Soph." Meaning, "I want to remind you of the existence of the dog so you will walk her."

I was the first one at The Greens. One other woman showed up, about my age with yellow hair, and the two of us rolled all the bikes out and lined them up in front of the door: instant bike parade, just add residents. Susanna handed out the buck slips. She said, "Dennis' dad died last night so if you get him it might be rough. Do your best to cheer him up."

I looked at my buck slip: Ride #1: Dennis.

Dennis turned out to be the friendly guy with the

wide face and big eyes whose shoe I had unstrapped on the last ride. I thought I might mention my father had recently died too, that we had that in common, but it didn't come up. In fact, he seemed in a pretty good mood.

As we made the turn toward the Senior Center, Dennis said to me, "I'm an EMT and have training in CPR so if anyone needs help up ahead you can let me handle it."

I said, "Okay."

Dennis said, "I know Tug Halper."

"Me too."

"We have a new rose bush and I'd like to get a sign reminding folks about the thorns. Have you seen the flower garden?"

I told him I had not and we talked about what sorts of foods people grew in gardens and how it was always important to enquire about allergies before offering anyone food. At the water break Dennis skipped his drink in favor of checking to make sure the other riders were doing all right. He slowly made his way to each person and everyone told him they were fine, even the volunteers. He walked unsteadily, like a stout, wobbly chair, but he was confident and got around fine.

My second rider rider was No Pedal No Talk Dwayne. Only Susanna had some news as she walked him over to me.

"Dwayne has been pedaling," she said grandly. "He keeps his hands on his knees instead of the handlebars, but it's a start."

As we headed out, Dwayne did pedal *and* held on to the butterfly handlebars. It was hard to not feel 100% responsible for his turnaround: that my chill attitude toward conversing and not pedaling had reached him.

My last ride was with Always Interesting Sandra. That's how Susanna described her to me.

"Here's Always Interesting Sandra," she said when handing her off.

Always Interesting Sandra was in her late 60s and wore spangly shorts and a t-shirt, with lots of sunscreen on her face and arms. When she got near a volunteer, she pushed her cheek out and yelled, "Kiss me!" And people did. I decided when she stuck her cheek out to me I would be a good sport and go along with it. As it happens, we pedaled the whole loop but she never asked me for a kiss. We even sat on a bench together chatting about the weather. Jaycee walked past us and said, "Well, *hellooo* Miss Sandra! How are we doing today?"

Sandra pointed to me. "Is he your boyfriend."

Jaycee's entire face puckered. "No." She sounded like a teenager whose parents had accused her of planning to break curfew.

"Kiss me," Sandra called, and pushed her cheek toward Jaycee.

Back home I napped and was awoken when Madeleine called to ask where I was. I admitted to napping before I realized my error and got yelled at. I wasn't late though, Madeleine had just gotten out early for her early dismissal. I grabbed the cello and picked her up and we got taken right away at the ear doctor. Furg was in with us for 45 seconds *tops* as he looked in her ear and said the tube was still not ready to come out.

I drove a different route to Wired and we bickered a little because it did maybe take longer than normal. Wired was closed so we drove to Rockford Register Roasters, which Madeleine hated because of the poorly executed hipster decor, but she was a good sport and got a $4.50 drink with whipped cream. I gave her the key to the Jeep as we had arranged and she drove to cello while I walked to Carlyle to wait for Molly for our "night out." Got a window seat, a pint of Humulus, and started writing in my diary. Felt slightly dizzy and wondered if the ol' Meniere's was flaring up.

Watched a man trying to parallel park, doing a terrible job of it. All the guys in the bar hooted and pointed, but the driver was unaware. He had two wheels up the curb, then a long pause, went forward, bumped the car in front, then backed out of the space to try again- quite disgraceful. I wondered if men mocking parallel parking skills was the final brave space for men to openly judge masculinity. I never would have thought that except I had a pen in my hand and my notebook open and a beer and I liked to appear to be writing when I sat alone in bars. When the driver finally did get it right there was a murmur of disgusted relief and a conspiracy was hatched wherein we would all cheer when he walked in, but he didn't come into Carlyle. He crossed the street and went into horrible Taco Betty.

Molly showed up shortly as we had planned and she got a beer and I got a second. I was trying to catch up on the day's diary but also doing some distracted chatting.

She said, "Are you going to keep writing?"

I said, "I just want to finish today. Don't you have something to work on?"

She said she did and went to the car and got a yoga book which she read for about five minutes, then said, "Are you going to be writing the whole time?"

I closed my notebook and Molly started telling me about the principles of yoga. As she went along I started to take notes to make a point about the one sided nature of our conversation, but it seemed to only encourage her. Molly explained all the *padas* to me. The first few were interesting, but I was surprised that the later ones involved gaining super powers like invisibility and astral projection. As a perennial dilettante who has only taken a few classes, I had been under the impression yoga was a reasonable, even sophisticated endeavor.

Molly wanted to eat at Taco Betty despite my reminding her that it was terrible and they served beer in a plastic pint "glasses" which were sometimes piping hot out of the dishwasher. Nevertheless we were seated upstairs, the secondary, disappointing seating area. We each got one order of tacos and I got a beer. An order consisted of three tacos, which had to be the same ingredient. One was not allowed to order, say, two shrimp tacos *and* a pork taco. The bill was almost forty dollars for six tacos and one beer. The tacos were not nearly as good as the ones down the street at Los Portales, where six tacos and one beer might cost ten dollars if you got an expensive beer, and it came with the tackle-box of pickled vegetables and the food was delicious and each separate taco could have whatever you wanted in it.

We both were in a funk and it started to rain on the drive home, but as we pulled up to the house, Molly said we should "clean slate each other." That sounded good so I kissed her cheek and we ran through the downpour to the house where I ate two pieces of Ben's leftover

Home Run Inn pizza. I called it "Touch Down pizza." No one laughed.

A couple of weeks later I woke up to Molly talking to and about the dog. She said she thought she should go to Farm and Fleet and get Sophie a chew bone so Sophie "wouldn't think about her paw so much."

I said, "You should get one for yourself too."

Molly said, "That's really funny," and then she started crying.

Madeleine came out and we started the Mini Crossword puzzle but I stopped calling out clues when they began talking over me to each other and I finished it in 65 seconds.

My front wheel was flat on the Marrake$h, which was confusing as I had not ridden it since before the trip. Drove in "Madeleine's car." Stopped at the bank to deposit Ben's college refund check. Parked in The Greens parking lot and sat in shade until Jaycee showed up. We rolled the bikes out and Susanna introduced me to two new volunteers.

"This is Mark, a cyclist who lives in Dead Elm, and this is Cindy. Her father is a doctor at KSB. This is Dan. He just got back from riding his bike in the Netherlands."

"Denmark," I said, which ended the conversation.

I was happy to note my first rider would be Dennis, so I went ahead and moved the seat forward even before Susanna walked him out. When we looped around the Senior Center, Dom came jogging past on the path pushing Ruby in a stroller. I high-fived him as he went by.

"What's his name?" Dennis asked.

"Dominic. Do you know him?"

"Is he in law enforcement? Because you have to stay in good shape when you're in law enforcement."

"Teacher."

At the water break I pulled up alongside Mark, the cyclist from Dead Elm. Mark said, "Heya Dennis."

"Hi Mark. Do you know Dan?"

"Just met him," Mark winked at me.

Dennis leaned forward and cupped his hand as if to speak privately to Mark. "I'm worried about Barry." Dennis pointed to the kid Mark was partnered with. "Barry doesn't sign as good as he should and I'm the only one who really understands him. If you need help with anything he says…"

Mark chuckled. "I think I got it Dennis, but thank you."

"You're going to be okay, Barry. You. Will. Be. Okay." Dennis was speaking tenderly like a parent, but Barry didn't seem to be paying attention. I unstrapped Dennis' feet from the pedals and helped him down.

Susanna was riding with a client too, and Dennis approached her with his cup of water. "Sorry dear, but I think we need to open a work order for the wheel on the third bike. It's got a hitch when we pedal."

"Thanks for letting me know, Dennis." Susanna looked at me. "Which wheel?"

I had no idea what Dennis was talking about. "The front one," I said. "Driver side." Dennis didn't correct me.

When the jug of water was empty, Barry wandered on to my bicycle. Since Dennis was talking to Mark, the cyclist from Dead Elm, I buckled Barry in and Dennis got on Mark's bike. Now that I was riding with Barry, Dennis turned his focus to me.

"Let me know if you need help understanding his signs," Dennis called to me while Mark velcroed his feet. "I'm the only one who understands him."

Barry didn't say anything except when I pedaled going downhill and we picked up speed, he waved his fists in the air and yelled *wheeee*, which I had no trouble understanding.

I was asked to come on Thursday instead of Monday. Perfect weather, looked at the cows on Town Hall, had the Bluetooth speaker going in one of the bottle cages.

Life felt just fine as I pedaled at a regular commuter's pace. Was passed by Tug Halper in his pickup truck twice as he drove back and forth on Highway Two and was tooted at, but only the first time. Got to The Greens and rolled the bikes out by myself. Susanna came out with a beefy guy, sunglasses on his visor, Cubs t-shirt. She said, "Dan, this is Bert."

We shook hands. "Really sorry to hear about coach McNair passing. I was in school the same time as the girls. Bridget and I had a lot of friends in common." He rattled a bunch of names, none of which I knew.

Bert said, "I heard Bridget is a pastor's wife. Is your church near here?"

I told him Molly was the one I was married to.

He looked thunderstruck. "The cheerleader?" He put his hand up to block the sun and get a better look at me.

Susanna led the riders from the building and we paired up and strapped down. Always Interesting Sandra wanted a bell on her handlebar and Susanna said it would have to be another time, but I said I had a tool in my bike bag and could do it. I took out the multi-tool from my frame bag on the Marrake$h and attached the bell, like Rick Moranis in the Night School High-Q sketch on SCTV. There was a sort of horrified look on Susanna's face when I finished, but Sandra dinged her bell the entire ride and had a great time. At the water break she asked Bert if I had a girlfriend.

"He's married," I heard him say.

"Aw, I'm always too late."

I wanted him to tell her it was to a cheerleader.

A middle aged woman with glasses was walking a small, yellow labrador past the picnic tables and the riders gathered around to pet the animal.

"Where are you all from," the woman asked. "The Greens?"

When Bert said, "Yes," she nodded and said, "That's what I thought," in an inscrutable but very specific way. The riders were crowding around her dog, who, she assured us, was a rescue. She wasn't helping us but she was useful too with the all the dog rescuing. As much as I hated this woman, the residents did enjoy the dog.

My second rider was Barry who waved his arms whenever I got going at a good clip so I tried not to drop under eight miles an hour, like a JoyRides Sandra Bullock. The third ride was with a loud, fun older woman named Clara who was flirting with Bert and when we stopped for water she insisted we switch. I took Bert's partner, a young woman with long, grey hair. As she was getting on she said, "Donut starts with D. D is for donut."

I thought, *this is going to be awesome,* but she didn't

say another word. She did pedal, hard, so we easily caught up to Bert, and as I passed them on the grass, Clara shrieked at us. I thought, *that's what you get for trading me*. I was really having fun!

Biked home. Stopped in the garden for some Swiss chard and pressed it into a grilled cheese. Molly texted me about getting beer for a cookout she had planned for her yoga students. I texted, "Get something standard that everyone will drink like Rolling Rock." She texted, "I'm at the grocery store in Scoldin. Do they have Rolling Rock here?" I did not bother to respond.

When Molly came home she told me she had not gotten the beer. She said "It's okay because I also forgot to get charcoal so you're going to need to go to the store anyway."

I said, "We have plenty of charcoal," but that was the end of the conversation.

I had an idea to write a nonfiction book about the Rock River based on my having biked the length of it with Radio's Carl Nelson, so I was reading an old book about the Sangamon River by Edgar Lee Masters, to get an idea about how a "river book" might be structured. While eating my two soft boiled eggs I read what Masters had to say about people he knew living near the Sangamon. He wrote about them romantically, sometimes slipping into verse right in the middle of a paragraph. He referred to a guy named Bill McNamar who never married and died in the poorhouse and who belonged to the "owls of Hartfield Woods." Sometimes Masters called Bill "the idiot of Sandridge," and the book had a drawing, depicting Bill as a kindly man with one eye closed and a corncob pipe, which he held in his mouth upside down.

Masters wrote, "It is possible that naturals like Bill have an understanding of nature and life so intimate and strange that they cannot express it. The look of Bill's eyes indicated that he was peering always into something that he had no words for."

I pedaled the Marrake$h to the final Monday of Joy-Riding with the residents at The Greens, where I brought all the bikes out by myself. Two volunteers drove up, a sullen mother daughter team, part of the the usual Monday crowd. The daughter said the rides "were killing" her mother. She unilaterally decided we wouldn't be going into the park and up the hill, instead we would pedal the residents to the Senior Center, but when Always Interesting Sandra heard, she complained to Susanna, so we cut a deal where we would go out to the park to the picnic tables, have water, then come back. It was half what we usually did, but double what the mother wanted.

Dennis was my first rider and we fist-bumped warmly when he stumbled away from Susanna. I was surprised to realize I appreciated Dennis; he wanted to be useful, which was something we had in common. As we pedaled toward Park West, a car went speeding past us on Pines Road. I said, "Probably some kid driving too fast."

Dennis said, "Maybe it's a volunteer fireman answering a call. You don't know what you'll find when you get there so you need to arrive pretty quickly." Dennis was kind and believed the best of people, which was something we didn't have in common. Dennis was the rider who made me most question my own reality. Sometimes I thought the only difference between me and the residents was that I chose to be there, but the truth was, Susanna told me when to ride and who to ride with, same as them. Maybe I was a member of a different Greens, a larger Greens where I was being kept busy inside a society I couldn't fathom. Was I sucking on some kind of upside down corncob pipe without knowing it?

I did two more rides, one with Gail who seemed to have forgotten about Sophie and never asked about her, and another with a man I had never met before. He pedaled. Because of the shortened routes we got done quickly, which was fine because it was a hot day. I put the bikes away by myself, the mother and daughter were inside the building chatting with people they knew, recovering from their arduous morning.

I biked home on the Marrake$h. Saw two cyclists having trouble at the side of the road by the golf course who turned out to be the Halpers waving off my offer of assistance. Jaycee had a pinch-flat and Tug was replacing the tube. When I got home I microwaved a hot dog, eating it with cucumbers in the Danish way. I texted Molly that we could go for a bike ride later if she wanted, ride out to Scoldin and get a beer like we had in Denmark. She did not want.

I keep writing. Not just about the Rock River, but I also have two completed novels I'm peddling. I spent eight years writing a novel in the third person and then, because of an offhand remark in a rejection letter, spent another year drafting a new version entirely in first person. No one is interested in publishing either version. I have good cover letters which always garner a response, requests for pages, the first ten, first fifty, first three chapters, and then things go cold. I am constantly sending queries and synopses to agents and editors. I submit short stories to literary journals by the dozens, scouring databases for new journals and magazines. I have stacks of rejection letters and get more and more each week. *Dear   , Greetings! Please find attached my story "Swiss Cheese Wednesday" which is 2,100 words long. It is a standalone piece of fiction but also part of a larger work of autofiction.* I bike down my driveway whenever I hear the mail truck going down Town Hall, even though I'm most likely to find another form rejection. The truth is, you don't know what you're going to find until you get there, and you may not know how to get there until you have arrived.

ART OF WARVILLE:
THE TWELVE LESSONS OF SUN TZU

Lesson One: Plan to be angry, keep your grudges at the ready. There are five ways to administer your grudge. They are:

By being immoral.

Madeleine and I headed out to her Suzuki lesson in the Jeep. Got mail. Excited to get my two pack of Woolie Boolies socks but when Madeleine opened them there was only one pair. My first thought was that I had accidentally only ordered one, but it said "2pk" right on the package Amazon sent. I wondered out loud if an employee had taken one of the pairs hoping I wouldn't notice, and this upset Madeleine, me blaming a worker. The conversation on the rest of the drive centered around what kind of an ass I am. (Can be a "big one," it turns out.)

Dropped her at Suzuki right on time and drove to Carlyle and had a beer. I hesitated because I had nothing to drink yesterday or Sunday, so if I also held off today that would be three alcohol-free days, which would make Wednesday's beer at Trivia that much better, but as I started drinking the pint of Humulus, I knew I had made the right decision.

The next day I went to UPS and handed off the single pair of socks to go back to Amazon. If only I could have talked to a human I would have told Amazon I'll keep the pair and they could send a second one or just refund half the money, however they wanted to handle it, but all I could do was send the socks and wait for a replacement set.

By being indiscriminate.

Daryl wanted to try the new trivia at Arrow. Jack and Daryl ordered food but Molly had made us eat at Natty's so we got to just watch them. We did okay, never super confident about any of the answers but still got a lot correct. One round was about coffee and I assumed we'd do great but neither Molly or I had heard of half the fancy coffee drinks, let alone how much milk or foam or whatever they required. We were sitting by the Moops and Bill said he thought Molly and I would get all the fancy coffee questions right. He didn't mean it kindly, although I was also surprised that Molly knew so few. Cortado we knew, but what's a cartadito? A piccolo? A cordusio? A gribralto? We're not even good at being snobs. Team came in a humiliating fourth place. Hawk Yeah came in first and Sharon stopped by to gloat on her way out. No one on Hawk Yeah drinks alcohol so they

get to leave while the rest of us are finishing our beers and settling our tabs.

Sharon said, "Hello friends."

I asked, "Why friends?" She usually calls us 'frenemies.'

Sharon said, "It represents growth." She did not specify on whose part.

By being capricious.

Molly and I did the mini puzzle and ran into trouble with the first clue, "Four letter word for Mad Libs command." We put "noun" but it turned out to be "verb" and it took at least 90 extra seconds longer to finish than it should have. In the afternoon Molly called and accidentally Facetime'd. It was hot to suddenly be looking at her. I asked her to pull her shirt down or flash something but she wouldn't. I pointed the camera toward my pants but she told me to stop. She had called to tell me about Dee, that her husband just had a significant stroke, the prognosis was not looking good. There was an unmistakable note of envy in Molly's voice.

By being out of accord with others.

Told Molly that I felt bad about how the last couple days of my mother's visit had gone, because I had been

short tempered and crabby. Molly responded by telling me all the things that bothered *her* about my mother's visit, which included how she constantly talks about the ills of old age and says "just you wait" after each one.

When Molly finished I said, "I'm glad I could get that off my chest."

She said, "Tell me what bothered you."

I told Molly I felt bad that I couldn't do what my mother wanted, which is to just have me focus on her and be enthralled with her every utterance, paying attention to everything she says with concern and adoration. That I couldn't just listen and respond with unconditional sympathy. That I didn't even say *'I love you'* when I dropped her off at the airport even though I knew she was waiting for me to.

Molly listened. When I was done she said she also didn't like that my mother had commented on Sophie's weight and that it made her feel defensive when my mother asked where things were in the kitchen because it's so disorganized.

By being immodest.

The sun came out very briefly and I walked around the lagoon on campus. It got warm so I unbuttoned my flannel shirt. Very attractive woman about my age walk-

ing in the opposite direction smiled at me as we passed one another. I couldn't figure it out. I thought briefly that maybe she liked me. Felt nice for a moment but then I remembered the shirt under my flannel was the Hop On t-shirt with the drawing of a hop on it, so she had probably just been amused by that. Felt relieved to understand the encounter correctly and also disappointed.

Lesson Two: A good grudge develops embryonically. Sometimes it's wise to temporarily forget the grudge for it to gestate into a viable, enduring resentment.

Up at 2am. Pee. Back to sleep. Wake up at 5:50am. Pee. Alarm goes off at 6:32am. Dream a joke about how at Luther College they post the cafeteria lunch menu by nailing it to the door. I might have dreamt that joke because I had a Toppling Goliath beer right before bed and they are in Decorah, Iowa, same as Luther College. I bet that explains the awkward, not-at-all-fun-to-say biblical name the brewers chose for themselves. I wonder, now that Toppling Goliath beer is everywhere, if they still think of themselves as a David. Thought about posting that musing on Facebook, but when I logged on, all the women were posting about sexual harassment. Doesn't seem like the right time for me to make a joke about beer.

Sat at the table and talked to Molly who was thinking about taking the dog to vet. Sophie has been itchy. We're out of milk so I gave the cat a flake of leftover salmon. Madeleine came out of her room and we did the Daily Mini Crossword. It took awhile because I put "man" for the clue "___ of steel," and it turned out to be "abs." Molly talked about yoga and how happy she is with her Monday morning class. We tried to think of a girl to fix Noel up with if he is going to stay much longer. Molly said she is depressed and thinks it's because of the gloomy weather. I reminded her that twenty seconds prior she had told me how happy she was with her yoga class. "That's true," she said, and seemed to brighten. Madeleine walked around the kitchen while brushing her teeth. I made a joke about how fashion models should brush their teeth while walking on the runaways, like if they're doing a line of pajamas for stay-at-home work people. I thought, "That's a good one for Facebook," but maybe not today.

Opened chicken coop. One egg on the ground, one egg in the nest. Cleaned the wading pool for the ducks, filled water trough. Molly texted from the waiting room of the vet to ask if we could invite her mom and Noel to dinner. I texted, "sure." She texted, "Can you do it?" Before going to school, I answered some emails. Beetee sat on my keyboard and I thought it would make a good photo for Facebook, but when I opened the app, everybody was still talking about sexual harassment. It seemed like everyone had a story. Some just posted, "me too," no other text. Others provided details, like they were walking down the road and a man honked at them. A student from last semester had a long post saying "since all women" have been harassed, it stands to reason that "all men are perpetrators." Not me, I thought. But then it occurred to me I may have done that horn honking thing once or twice.

In computer lab, Omar challenged my claim that *The Faraway Brothers* is the first book ever published by an author with the first name "Lauren." I acted surprised and told him he should send me an email, and if he used MLA to cite his source, I would give him extra credit. Omar didn't have the handbook so I showed him how to use the Purdue Online Writing Lab site to get the citation formatted correctly, which is how I ended up accidentally teaching something today.

Tekiah walked in late, about halfway through the class, and said she wanted to talk to me privately. We walked into the corridor. Last week Tekiah wore a red, low-cut crop-top, with the words "No More Fuckboys" in big white letters. I don't remember what she was wearing this afternoon, but not that. Tekiah told me she was worried about Marissa because no one had seen her since yesterday. She said Marissa is seeing a guy who is "really sketchy," and Marissa's roommate texted that she didn't come home yesterday. Tekiah asked me what she should do. Should she call the cops?

I told Tekiah that I had gotten an email from Marissa kind of recently. Tekiah actually hopped up on the balls of her feet and wanted to know what it said. I hesitated. "I can't really tell you what it says because of the FER-PA privacy rules." Really, I hadn't read it carefully and didn't remember.

I checked my phone and scanned the message. Marissa had written she wasn't feeling well and would miss class and did I want her to send what was due via email. I had answered, "Thanks for letting me know and send the work if you can, if not you can show me Monday in class." This was a relief because if something happened to Marissa, this email would become part of the public record and I seemed like a perfectly reasonable, almost caring person, although other teachers would know I was clearly encouraging her to not turn in the work so there would be less for me to do. I also didn't come off as "overly interested," which would have thrown suspicion on me, depending on what happened to Marissa.

I told Tekiah that Marissa's email came at 11am, "Ninety minutes ago, so she's probably okay."

Tekiah said, "That's a lot later than anyone else has heard from her."

I felt weirdly honored by that; hashtag, look who's an ally.

Tekiah sat down at the only empty computer terminal and I continued class. I had them pulling direct quotes out of Larry King interview transcripts, and changing them into paraphrased indirect quotes. After a short while Tekiah got upset again, and waved me over. She said she just got a text from Marissa. They have a code with a "safe word" and an "unsafe word" and Marissa just texted her the unsafe word. "Is it okay if I go check on her?"

I said, "Absolutely! Do you want me to contact the police?"

To my great relief, she said, "No. I got this."

I said, "Let me know if you need me to do anything." I was loud so that everyone in the room could hear in case we got deposed.

While I was driving home thinking it over, the one thing I wished I had done differently was to have asked

Tekiah what the what the two code words were. Just out of curiosity.

Lesson Three: Break your grudges into multiple pieces. Any attempt at reconciliation with your adversary will thus be incomplete.

I drove to town and parked the car across from Mabel's Barber Shop. Another guy was parking his sedan so I rushed to get into the barbershop before him, but he beat me by a full stride. I went back for my book and discovered I had left the car running. A third car pulled up so I again rushed to the door, this time stepping into a sizeable slush puddle.

Mabel knew the guy before me in line and also the guy who came in after me, and they talked while I pretended to read. She knew me too, but only as a customer. The three of them used lots of colorful phrases, such as, "She's tighter than a second coat of paint," which was used by the guy-after-me to describe his wife's cheapness and why he was surprised she still let him "take" the Rockford newspaper. Mabel said it would be, "Colder than a well digger's ass," in reference to the temperature tomorrow.

When it was my turn in the chair, a fourth guy came in to wait. It was Tuesday, senior discount day. I noticed I was the only one who had left a puddle of melt-water on the floor, the other men had the decency to wipe their boots on the welcome mat. Mabel once told me that she loves two things in life: cutting men's hair and guns. The décor of her shop reflects these passions, with kitschy wood cutouts of old timey haircut joints, the kind Norman Rockwell might have painted, and sketches of pistols and revolvers. She likes me because once when we were talking about straight razor shaving—which she used to do but can't now because it's illegal—I had used the word "strop." Mabel told me she doesn't like that everyone says "strap," not that she would correct anyone. She said, "It hardly ever comes up anymore."

On my last visit, Mabel told me she was retiring soon, maybe in a year. She was waiting for her niece to finish barber school up in Rockford because you have to get so many hours in to get a license. She had said to me, "When my niece takes over, you guys are going to really love it. She's young. A real cutie."

I had two thoughts: First, it was embarrassing for Mabel to think she had to dangle her attractive niece like some Pigalle procuress. And second, I highly doubted she would be all that cute, we would have to see.

Today, Mabel was beginning my "one on the sides, finger length on top" when the next guy after me asked if anyone had heard anything about Harley Heartly, who had recently been struck by a car while riding his bicycle to work. Mabel tsked and said, "I told him! I may have to slap him myself, riding a bike on Daysville."

I said, "He was wearing a safety vest and had two lights," which I knew from Facebook.

Guy-After-Me said, "I don't understand why bikes are even *allowed* on the road. They don't pay no license and they block traffic."

Third Guy nodded. "I want to run them all over."

"I just might do that," Guy-After-Me said.

Mabel gave me a look in the mirror. Mostly what we talk about is my bike riding and we call the cut I get, "the bike helmet haircut." She had already said, "Now now now," a bunch of times trying to get both of them to shut up, but the conversation organically moved on its own, when Third Guy randomly wondered out loud if Trump was an only child.

I said, "He has a sister who's a judge." I did not add that Trump also had a brother who died from being a drunk because I didn't want to make it seem like I knew *too* much about Trump, and while I was sure these assholes had voted for him if they voted at all, Guy-After-

Me did call Trump's keeping the government closed, a "temper tantrum."

Next Guy wondered how much money Governor Pritzker had, and I feared things were about to get anti-you-know-what, so I was glad to have my haircut over and—after a bit of confusion where I only had a few singles in my wallet before remembering my emergency dub—I paid and tipped and left. I wondered how long it took Mabel to tell the guys that I was one of those bicycle riders they would soon be attempting to run over.

Lesson Four: A grudge is not cooling; a grudge is not a paper fan to be unfolded and waved. A grudge radiates heat, a grudge is a buried ember.

A list of irritating things about my father's illness and subsequent death:

That I first heard of his diagnosis in a group text in the middle of a Saturday when I was on a two day bike ride with the Quad City people. Some of the numbers on the massive text thread were people I didn't know, some were people I did know and didn't like.

That after some gallows humor was exchanged privately between my brother and me, I went back on a larger family text and made a pretty mild joke. My brother responded in the family thread that I got the award—along with Iris—for the best "deflection." Iris, the person he says had a response most similar to mine, was ten.

That a cousin I hadn't seen in decades sent super long texts to just our side of the family with her medical opinions. She agreed with the medical team's course of actions, said the new medicines had shown "incredible results." Although her day job was that of a manager of mobile pet groomers, she regularly peppered her texts with words like "induction," and "contraindicated," and "protocols." Her final assessment was that "dad" (which is how she started referring to my father, as though she was our social worker) should "remain tranquil."

That my dad's wife sent out a call for memories for something she calls "Operation Jokes and Hope to Cope." I had to use my fingers to physically keep my eyeballs from rolling into my forehead. His wife's idea, that we all come up with jokes and inspirational sayings to share to his Facebook page, made me feel competitive and resentful. Not looking at his Facebook page was the cornerstone to my plan for keeping myself from getting irritated. I had looked once, Molly actually encouraged it, and predictably it was full of the most horrible people saying the most ridiculous things imaginable about what a courageous battle my father was waging, mixed in with a bunch of puns.

That when his wife sent a text saying she feared we were nearing the end and everyone needed to get a last visit in, and she suggested some dates, I responded, "Any of those dates would be fine with me," which was followed by days of silence. I assumed she was getting all his new friends and new family squared away before slotting his old family. It even occurred to me that she had probably meant to put the call out to just their folk band friends but accidentally used Operation Jokes and Hope to Cope.

That I felt a pressure to get a visit in. That I had always felt in competition for my father's attention, from his work, from his colleague Nelson Pazminio's kids in Peru or Brazil or wherever—the ones I was told could "run rings around me," (they could dive off a board while I was still in basic swimming, never able to advance), and now mostly from his wife's family who seemed to adore him.

That in the end, I knew I would end up feeling bad about either showing too much affection or not enough.

That I was on my bike riding near the S curve on Grist Mill Road east of Chana when my mother called to tell me the news. It wasn't our regularly scheduled call time so I knew what it was as soon as I saw her name. I got off my bike and answered.

That later, when I would lead bike rides to show new people the area, when we were riding down Grist Mill, I would say, "We're coming up on Dead Man's Curve. It's not dangerous, it's where I was when I learned my father died."

That no one ever laughed.

Lesson Five: Where institutional disorder exists, a grudge allows individual order.

Went to Silage Hall for the Cultural Sensitivity Seminar. This was just for DSU instructors, all 140 of us. The

Professorial Tenured and Tenure-Track faculty—with their good thinkin' brains n' caring spirits—were not required to attend. My English colleagues had already commandeered one of the round tables: Daphnie, Marla, Kate, Helen, all of them. I had planned on sitting by myself so I could daydream, but was waved over and took the only remaining seat, which was between Tess and Janice. Because my back was to the podium, I used the excuse of not wanting to twist my back all afternoon to move to an empty table. I did this in the nick of time: as I settled in, Edith Lifesuck floated in under a billowing caftan and took the seat I vacated. A man from Thailand who taught in Foreign Languages and a busty woman from COMS eventually joined me, and we three spread out around a twelve person table, all able to face the lectern.

We had one speaker for the full four hours: stately plump Marci Mulligan, who started out by telling us that she's often asked by white people, "Where are you from?" The room gasped. Marci assured us she responds only with a withering glance toward the offensive questioner. (Later she told us she had been born in Costa Rica, but not because any of us asked.) Marci said the same people who want to know where she's from are surprised to learn her husband is a "six foot tall, white man with red hair." We didn't gasp this time, but Marci let that sit a few seconds before asking if anyone had any questions. I didn't have to turn around to know Edith Lifesuck's hand was up. She's our "any questions" running back, so good at spotting openings that she often has her hand up before the speakers begin soliciting them. This time she began, "As a mother of a child with a non-debilitating physical impairment…" before pivoting to thank the organizers and the speakers on behalf of the audience. I did not feel thankful but I don't know how the other 139 instructors felt, most of whom were applauding in agreement with Edith. My assumption was that the Cultural Sensitivity Seminar would mostly waste my time, but also that I would learn something, glean some new terms or practices which would be useful.

Marci passed out some handouts, and I realized my glasses were missing. I texted Finn Lee, who confirmed they were on the floor of his office by the chair I had been sitting in before the seminar, killing time. A few more texts and the promise to buy him a beer, and he said he would walk them over by the first break. I refused to eat any of the cookies on principle.

After break, Marci gave us "space" to learn about ourselves. One exercise had us write down eight groups that "identify" us. I dutifully wrote white and straight and Jewish and all the things I thought I was supposed to write. Next we were to cross off two of the labels. We were never told what criteria to use or why, and when some instructors from a nearby table asked for clarification, Marci explained, "Two of them."

Another exercise was to list emotions we felt when we had been "excluded." Then we were to discuss with our table-mates. The Thai man, busty COMS woman, and I shared our words. We all had "hurt" and "frustrated." I was the only one who wrote "irritated" but the COMS woman agreed that was a good one. Marci returned to the podium, and with all the panache of a birthday party mentalist, revealed that the words we had shared had been negative. She nailed it! Now she directed us to think about a time when we had been "included" and talk about how that felt. Lo and behold, everyone at my table felt better about those times. The COMS woman had written "happy" and so had I, and amazingly so had the man from Thailand, and English wasn't even his first language! Marci mingled, going from table to table, and when she got to us, the woman from COMS told her it would be great to talk about *how* to make people feel more included in our classrooms. Marci agreed, but it never came up.

During the second cookie break where my resolve to not eat the snacks crumbled and I filled a small plate with a half dozen, I talked to my tablemates. The man from Thailand said he was a Buddhist which allowed these "micro-aggressions" to roll off his back. He said, "People don't intend to be hurtful," when they say dumb things so it didn't bother him. Then he took out his phone and showed me a picture of his two daughters lounging poolside in bikinis. They were stunning: early twenties, sweet smiles, cleavage. Was this a trap? My mind raced for something neutral to say, *Is that your pool?* Or, *I bet they're nice to their friends.* My throat tightened at the thought of trying to muster the proper tone until whatever was the right amount of time to look at a stranger's daughters, I had gone way past. Fortunately, just then the COMS woman glanced at the phone and said, "Jesus Christ, they're gorgeous!"

At 4pm, Marci asked the group, "What time do we go till?"

I called out, "Four o'clock!"

Marci said, "Perfect, we're nearly done."

But there was some laughter, and Edith and a few other nervous instructors yelled corrections, that actually we weren't done until 5pm.

Marci seemed confused but when she finally understood that we had another hour, she said, "Oh okay, I can go until five."

And she did! Despite being nearly done, she managed to hold the floor another hour.

The English department has a staff meeting before the start of every fall semester. The head of First Year Composition calls it so the Grad Students, who will each take one section of 25 students, can learn about the program. Also required to attend are the instructors, who every semester teach four sections, a total of 100 students. At my first meeting I learned some things and found it pretty useful. I have since been required to attend 23 more of these meetings. The Professorial Tenured and Tenure-Track Faculty, noggins chock full o' sagacity n' perception, are not required to attend, and don't.

We meet in a lecture hall. Richard May starts with a rundown of the basic rules: copy requests need to be made a week in advance, contact the program coordinator if you're going to cancel a class, lock the shared offices when you step out, the secretaries are busy so try not to bother them by asking questions or by saying "good morning."

The first guest speaker is always the textbook rep. She coaches us on how to use the expensive grammar handbook students are required to buy. The books are tough to use and tougher to teach from because every year the publisher changes the way they are laid out to keep incoming students from being able to buy cheaper, used copies. We are also told what to say when students ask certain questions, such as "Isn't all this available free online?" We are not supposed to say, "Yes."

The textbook rep also buys us lunch: wrapped half sandwiches from Panera. Led by Edith Lifesuck, we applaud in gratitude. It is the only food provided to non-tenured or non-tenure-track faculty all year long, and we lifers know to take two, which is why instructors stand in line with our *bouches*.

The afternoon is reserved for ice-breaking and "break-out sessions." This year the after-lunch speaker was none other than Cultural Sensitivity Instructor, stately plump Marci Mulligan! Although the instructors had already spent four hours Monday being trained on sensitivity, the Grad Students had not. Molly had ditched the meeting Monday to no consequence, so the material was new to her. Marci passed out the CORNS sheets and began with her stock anecdotes of her getting the upper hand on micro-aggressors: the video clerk who assumed she couldn't carry all her rentals and attempted to hand her a tote bag (probably not a recent event but still illustrative), the woman at the grocery store who asked where she was "*from*," whose mouth dropped when she saw Marci's "six foot tall, white husband with red hair." The Grad Students happily jumped in with their stories. One woman said she would outright ban the word "Trump" in her classroom for any reason. Another had "breast cancer issues" and so would not allow any research topics involving health care as it would be triggering. Sandy, an instructor who had been through this before, helpfully reminded us that just because someone looked white they might not be. She cited "holocaust people" as an example of someone who might look white but really wasn't. She clarified that she herself was not a "holocaust person," but warned that you never knew who might be.

Not one student in any of my three First Year Composition classes had the textbook on the first day and someone reported the bookstore had none. Despite the rain, before the third class I crossed campus to verify at the student center. The shelves were empty and the employees behind the counter were in loud, heated conversation—complete with easy expletives—about how much they hated their boss. One of them said she didn't actually hate him, but if she heard his fucking voice on the phone asking about a book one more time, she would kill him. It sounded like she meant it.

The first student to stand in the third class when I had them introduce themselves was named Tavio, and before he could say anything else, a student named James asked, "What kind of Mexican are you?"

Before Tavio could answer, Shelly scolded James from the back of the room. "That's rude!" she shouted. "They don't like that!"

James said, "I'm asking because you don't say Mexican if they're from Puerto Rico."

Shelly wasn't having it. She said, "What kind of Black are you? How do you like that question?"

He said, "Nigerian! That's what kind of Black I am. What kind of Black are you?"

Shelly said, "American!"

"Good for you." James turned to the still standing Tavio and asked, "So what kind of Mexican are you?"

Tavio said, "Puerto Rican."

I stood during all of it wondering if I should step in and do something. They were sitting in the new, ergonomic swivel chairs and somehow all the swiveling made it so no one was really facing me, and anyway everyone was smiling and laughing and no one seemed upset. At this point I did say, "In two weeks someone is coming in to give us Sensitivity Training so let's hold off on any further questions about what kinds we are until we get trained on how to ask."

A woman stuck her head in my office door and asked where the bathroom was. I said, "You have to go down to nine." When she left, I realized the ninth floor only has female bathrooms and by assuming this woman identified as female, I had committed a hate crime—as I type this sentence, I keep removing modifiers. I originally wrote, "basically committed," and "inadvertently committed," but I need to recognize the toxic brainwashing and give myself some ~~safe~~ brave space to acknowledge what happened (not "what happened," what *I did*) and learn from it. Thinking of my CORNS worksheet, I could have contained my presuppositions about where I should have directed her by being open to her nonverbals before speaking from my own experience.

"The tenth floor has no bathrooms," I should have said. "The ninth floor has a facility labeled "female" and the eighth floor has "male." If you would like to use a gender neutral bathroom you can go to the bottom floor, walk across the stone garden to Beeswing Hall, go to the second floor and wait three weeks for the school to get the hefty bags over the urinals and the scheduled re-opening of that facility, but don't bring it up in front of the English Department Council."

Weeks into the semester, all of my classes get a visitor: stately plump Marci Mulligan! It has been decided English class is where the University will bestow cultural sensitivity upon the student body, but in classes taught by instructors only. The rest of the undergrads will be sensitized via proximal osmosis from their Tenured or Tenure-Track Professors, those tweedy bodhisattvas, those comfy shoe'd saints. Marci is already in the classroom when I arrive. She has written out the principle of CORNS on the whiteboard.

C-Contain your pre-supposes

O-Open, be open to others

R-React with awareness

N-nonverbals should be paid attention to

S-Speak only from your own experience

The students are told to take a picture of it with their phones and to "favorite" the photo so it's always accessible.

For an icebreaker, Marci tells the class to high five one another, say what their "go to snack" is, and recommend a movie. Our ice has been broken for a long time now, but maybe this is for Marci, although she does not participate. She does ask me what time class ends, which I know from experience is both crucial and irrelevant.

We commence training, which consists of Marci

asking a provocative question, then clumping us into groups based on our answers. Is everyone who voted for Trump racist? Is Black Lives Matters more important than All Lives Matter? One corner is designated, "strongly agree," another is "somewhat agree," across the room we have "strongly" and "somewhat" disagree. Once we're in our respective corners, Marci directs us to explain our thinking. In answer to a student's question, Marci says Black people can't be racist but they can be prejudiced. This seems to be cheering news to everyone. She also tells them to put their phones away but hangs on to hers and texts from time to time.

My second class is combined with Lucy's students from across the hall, and they troop in, making appreciative noises about our ergonomic swivel chairs. We go through the ice breakers: Marci tells the crowd her "best go to snack," and a few of the students gamely offer up theirs. This is my lively class, and as soon as Marci mentions Trump and BLM, the students start talking over each other, arguing. One of my students calls Trump a successful businessman, which kind of breaks my heart.

Amelia says, "I wish some white kids were doing this with us too."

Jolene corrects her, "Caucasian."

A student from Lucy's class says, "Why are only colored people here?"

Marci jumps in. "People first. We don't say colored people. We say people of color."

"Then why is it 'white people?'"

I notice during this go-round Marci's prompts change during the discussion. She starts with "Everyone who voted for Trump is racist," but once we're in our response corners she says, "Everyone who *supports* Trump," and by the end of the discussion she's saying, "Everyone *who will* vote for Trump." For me anyway, all three versions have different answers.

Marci asks if we think people with disabilities have it hard on campus, citing the "cut-outs" in the sidewalk. She had used this one with the Grad Students, so I wasn't surprised to hear the prompt, or her explanation about what a "cut out" is.

"Cut-out," she repeats.

"The cracks?"

"No. A cut-out. In the sidewalk. The cut-outs."

Eventually the students stop asking and just agree cut-outs are a problem.

It's during the third class that the ice really breaks and Marci elaborates that the movie she recommends has "good acting." I like thinking about Marci Mulligan sitting on her couch with her tiny legs and four kids and her red haired husband and a big plate of cheese and sliced sausages (her favorite go-to snack) watching Netflix, appreciating the "acting." When people say "good acting" they just mean it has a cast with people they have already heard of.

This time, when we get to the question about Trump voters, Taylor in the front row says, "I want to hear what Libman has to say."

I defer, but Marci says. "Go ahead."

So I say, "Okay, but my opinion is not more valid than anyone else's," which I can't even make sound like I even remotely believe so I hurry on to the next part. "But, well, it seems to me, one could *maybe* say *it's possible* some people were ignorant about what Trump was three years ago, but we've had so much of his bullshit since then. We all know what he is and if you're still supporting him, to me that's racist."

Huge applause; the only applause of the afternoon. Taylor yells, *this is why you're my favorite teacher.* Marci quiets the class down and has Lucy answer the question too and I think she says something more empathetic, though I can't hear it over the sound of my own throbbing pleasure.

On my drive home two things bother me: The first

is how many students believe "being a billionaire" is a good thing, something to be lauded instead of being a sign of sociopathy.

Second, during the last class, one of Lucy's students had asked me if he could use the bathroom. I said, "Of course," instead of pointing out that Marci was in charge and his own teacher was also in the room. Was it because I was the only white adult present? Maybe something about my nonverbals? And why did I answer at all? How did that make Marci and Lucy feel? Maybe on some level I felt like I should be in charge. This shit's hard to shake.

Daryl and I were the only two at trivia that night. We sat at the corner of the bar and drank our beer and answered the questions. I like that we sit at the bar when some of other teams, Smarty Pants and Shaken Bacon, sit at the low tables like they're in a family restaurant instead of a bar in a bowling alley. But of course, Smarty Pants is made up of older women. It is probably easier for them to manage with the low chairs. And one of the Shaken Bacon guys is wheelchair bound. He can only reach a low table. Maybe they want to sit at the bar too, but here they are, Team Shaken Bacon, with all their noxious politics, taking a low table so their friend in the wheelchair can join them every week. One of them takes him to and from the bathroom, and another guy holds the door for him and makes sure he can negotiate the cut outs (I'm guessing). Would I ever behave so thoughtfully? Sometimes I talk to the guy in the wheelchair, I don't even know his name, and I'm wishing someone would take a picture so I could put it on Facebook. The caption would be, "Another fun night at trivia," but really I would want people to see me talking to a man in a wheelchair, like it's something I actually do all the time.

Lesson Six: A well nurtured grudge is a tide that lifts all ships. A grudge has a crest and a grudge has a trough, but the grudge is immutable.

Up at 12:15am with a pain in my left jaw and ear so bad I feel like crying when I swallow. Get up and look for Tylenol and find a bottle of something called Excedrin which I think has Acetaminophen in it but I'm not wearing glasses. If I hold it up to the oven light and stretch my arm, I can make out a long word beginning with A. Also that it expired in 2010. In the same cabinet is a bottle with Tylenol crossed off and in sharpie someone has misspelled Benadryl over it. All this is to say I'm not super confident about what I am holding but I take it anyway. Back to bed. Up at 3:23am to pee and this time

I realize I am in a lot less pain. In seems to have almost gone away. Drift back off to sleep.

I make two groundsy mugs of coffee and Molly is nice about it. Open coop, feed and water hens. Take off boots and Molly says, "Lets do the puzzle." It's just the two of us and I assumed we only did the Crossword Mini to have an activity which involved the kids, but I guess there is more to it. Eggs and toast. Madeleine has to go in early so I pull the car 'round and wait in the passenger seat. Text Madeleine to not forget her learner's permit. As she drives we talk about how everyone in Cole Ridge is deeply in love with anything related to law enforcement and the military. I told her how I had seen on Facebook some of the parents are starting a petition asking that the school *start* random drug testing. They *want* their kids handing over urine to their teachers. *"Dead Elm and Scoldin already do it,"* one mom wrote. *"It's not fair to our kids!"* When we pulled up to the pool doors a guy in an FBI ball cap walked past the car and seemed to give us the eye. Madeleine said we shouldn't be talking like this in public and headed into the building.

Took more ibuprofen, Dr. Skate was busy but I managed to snag an appointment with the Advanced Practice Nurse. Before sitting down in the waiting room I asked the receptionist if I could mute the TV. "Since I'm the only one here."

She said, "I'll just turn it off," and waved the remote.

I said, "Even better," and sat down. Since she seemed like a kindred spirit, I called out, "That must drive you nuts all day having that on."

She said, "I can't really hear it back here. Do you have a more up to date insurance card? This one got declined."

I said I didn't and she said not to worry, that "it" happens sometimes. Was unclear how insurance can be denied, since it's not like a credit card and the ramifications are a much bigger deal, but decide not to pursue further conversation.

Was led into an examining room I had never been in by a nurse I had never seen, both unusual since we've been with Dr. Skate since Ben was born. I enjoy being asked questions like, "Do you use any opioid products" and "Do you use tobacco including snuff or vape products" because it feels good to have someone interested. Terry Gross should start every interview asking the guest how many recreational drinks they consume a week and what their pain level is on a scale of one to ten. When the nurse asks about my pain level I always downplay it, calling a six a four so I don't look like a hypochondriac. I figure a four seems significant and you get the same level of attention as a six, but don't look like a baby.

While describing my symptoms I used the word "expectorate" because I wanted the nurse know she needed to be on her game. My blood pressure was 135 over 79 measured by cuff over shirt, my temperature was 97.9 measured via a wand rubbed against my forehead, and my oxygen level, 97%, measured via a fingertip sensor.

I said, "I've never had my oxygen level measured before. What does 97% mean?"

She said she didn't really know but she didn't think it was possible to have one hundred percent so 97 was probably good. "Most people ask me how we measure oxygen through the finger tip, but I don't know the answer to that either."

We stopped talking at that point except for when she swabbed my throat and I gagged. She said, "You really didn't want me in there."

I didn't have to wait long before the Advanced Practice Nurse, a kind woman about my age in a white doctor's smock, walked in. She said her name was Robin and began touching my face and neck to feel my glands. She pressed under my jaw and said, "I like your watchband because…" And then there was a word I didn't catch. She may have said "green" or a kind of green or I might just think she said that because the watchband is green.

I said, "Thanks, it's new," and I wanted to say I got it so I wouldn't look at my phone so much but she started asking about how much pain I was in.

I said, "Four," hoping she would understand I was downplaying.

It turned out I didn't have strep. Robin thought I had a bronchial infection and recommended I use a nasal spray. I said I had never used one but my wife had a neti pot.

Robin said, "Nice to know your wife is good for something, right?" It took me by surprise. I was going to say, *No no, we have a good marriage. A loving relationship,* but instead I just chuckled and said, "Right."

I left with a prescription for antibiotics. As I was putting on my coat in the vestibule I wondered if I could jog this afternoon. I asked the receptionist if I could walk back and ask one more question. She seemed stunned and said she wasn't sure. "It's just a quick question," I assured her. The receptionist picked up the phone and turned her body and spoke in a low voice.

"Tell her it's about exercise, if she thinks I can do some today."

The receptionist hung up and said I could go back in the examining room, which I did. I sat for awhile, I assume as a punishment, and when Robin came back I was very apologetic. "I was just wondering if you thought I could work out today. I tried to ask over the phone but..."

"Definitely exercise if you can, but take it down to about 80% for awhile." I thanked her and said I would be back in if I thought of anything else. She didn't laugh.

Drove home. Noticed Satellite radio had been enabled for a week of free holiday promotion. The Satellite radio coming on for free is the second best day of car radio ownership, the first best day is a week later when they turn it off again. Went though Snyder's in Cole Ridge for my prescription but the woman said they were backed up and it would be another 45 minutes so I went home. Got mail. Saw that the wind had blown the coop closed and opened it. Changed into running costume and ran to Highway Two and back, which is about 60% of my long workout but 100% of my short one. Came back and watched a brief documentary on Pornhub about how unscrupulous landlords take advantage of their tenants. Walked dog. Fed the horses Ate the last leftover chicken wing from Chili Pepper and threw out a bunch of stuff going bad, including two moldy tomato sauces and a baggie of something organic that was just brown sludge.

Got text Madeleine was ready to be picked up. Stayed in driver's seat because she didn't want to be driving if we were going through pharmacy drive thru lane. Madeleine said my texts to her had repeated four times on her phone. As she was saying this, it came in a fifth time.

Went to Snyder's and got the prescription. Was asked if I needed counseling and when I said I did not, I was told to press a button on a screen which said, "I decline counseling." We listened to a Barbara Streisand song on the Broadway station. I said we could think about subscribing for real but Madeleine said not to bother. I had already caught three Pearl Jam songs on three different stations in just a few hours and was wondering how people could stand paying for it. Maybe nobody actually does. Madeleine said, "Let's enjoy it for a week and then miss it until next year." Got a call from Molly asking if she should buy a rotisserie chicken. I said she should not because I was making pasta and beans and a salad. Took ibuprofen. Molly came home with a rotisserie chicken.

Took first antibiotic. We watched a Great British Bake Off in which Nadiya fucked up the show stopper and cried, but Paul and Mary told her the flavors were good. It was clear she wouldn't be cut because another dude had fucked up worse but we were nervous anyway. Paid the Com Ed bill. Remembered music rental bill and paid that while Madeleine played piano. I drank a beer, took a Tylenol. Let Beercat in window. Went out and sealed the dryer vent for the night with clothes pins, running the dryer for a few seconds first to scare off any mice. Turned off lights, locked doors, took off ring, talked to

Molly, powered down computer, turned on alarm, peed, brushed teeth, went to bed. Pulled sheet across bed but could not quite tuck in because Molly was already asleep.

Lesson Seven: Grudges anneal, a worthwhile grudge is generational, dynastic.

My mother called. She wanted to know what the weather is supposed to be in Chicago next weekend because she is going to Buffalo, New York, to visit my brother and his family and doesn't know how to dress. When I paused, she says the weather is about the same in Buffalo as it is in Chicago. She agreed my suggestion to, "Look it up on the internet," was a good one. I also suggested she save a step by looking up Buffalo instead of Chicago.

My mother called. She wanted to know what CDR means, and when I asked for context, she said a CDR is a CD that doesn't work in her CD player. She said Face-book sometimes says she likes stuff without her ever having said so.

My mother called. Lots going on health-wise: Herb had just fallen. He won't accept live-in help or any kind of assistance despite living in a two-story house and has balance issues due to Parkinson's. Later in the call she said, "Herb just fainted." She had gotten text from Herb's daughter. Still won't go over because doctors might come and remove him anyway and then he won't be there. She's pretty sure Herb broke a hip this time. (Based on same text.)

My mother called. She said things were really primitive at Ghost Ranch where she just spent the weekend. When I said I didn't know where Ghost Ranch was located, she asked me if I had ever heard of Georgia O'Keefe. Ghost Ranch didn't have a lot of food—not known for it, in fact *known* for *not* having a lot of food. At Ghost Ranch her book, "Hanie's Sad Secret" won first place in the Inspirational category and third place in the Young Adult category. She had entered the same book in both categories. I asked if there were fees to enter. She read notes from both judges whom she agreed with me were probably women, based on the references to tears being shed while reading the book. (Seemed like Inspirational judge cried more.) Couldn't answer my question about whether YA judge was an actual "Young Adult."

My mother called. Had already called once this week, but this was a bonus call for Ben's birthday. After she wished him well, I got handed the phone. She said her Comcast is out so no internet but she can see one station on each television—the last channel she was watching on each one. She has three TVs so she can see PBS, CBS, and Comedy Central. I said, "I guess that means you can still watch Big Bang Theory." She said, "Only when it's on."

My mother called. Wanted to know how my classes were going. I lost my temper. I shouted that she has asked me that every week for twenty years. "What exactly do you want to know? Attendance? Test scores? What could I possibly tell you about my classes that would mean anything to you?" She said the right things, that she was just making conversation, but I couldn't calm down. "You're going to ask me again next week, so tell me, what is it you want to know?" She said she just wanted to talk to me.

My mother called. She read a list of things Facebook says Ben has "liked" to see if he really liked them. I said he must have, but I did think some of them, like Walmart and Buffalo Wild Wings seemed dubious.

My mother called on Tuesday because I requested the weekly calls be moved back to Sunday. Actually, the original request was not to have a specific weekly obligation, that we should talk, "Only when either of us has something to say. " Sunday she called and I didn't answer. Monday she called and I didn't answer but I called back and she didn't answer. Hence the Tuesday call. She said she was going on a train trip across Canada to research her new book, "Hanie Takes a Vacation," so she wouldn't be around when I had my root canal but I should still call if there was an emergency. I told her I couldn't envision an emergency during root canal where I would ever need to call her. Might the dentist drill through my gum and suddenly need to know about Herb's latest fainting spell? She also said there would be limited email and WiFi available and she had pre-paid for international cell coverage but was concerned there might be limited connectivity because it was Canada.

As it turned out, I got an email from her on Thursday wishing me luck with the root canal and another on Friday expressing hope that the root canal had gone well.

My mother called on Saturday to say she's back from Canada and just dropped Mac off at the airport in Albuquerque. (No idea, didn't ask.) She had a great time in Canada. Would move to Alberta in a heartbeat. Twice heard bus drivers announce to tours that Trump was building a tower in Canada and both times everyone booed. (She thinks Canadians are under the impression Americans would be excited about that.)

I called my mother. She told me she saw a picture of Miya and Madeleine on Facebook but doesn't know how. I said it's because she's friends with them. She said she *is* friends with them but who can say why things appear on Facebook. I said, I can and I just did. She said they keep changing things and she's tired of it. She said she doesn't understand why people ride their bikes in groups because if one falls then everyone falls. I assumed she was worried about my trip, so I told her RAGBRAI isn't like the Tour de France. On RAGBRAI we're all spread out and going slow. I didn't mention the drinking. She said it sure *looks* like they ride close and fast when they ride along the highway by her. I said those guys were probably training to race which is not something I do. She said, "Sometimes they're going slow."

I realized there is an actual mathematical formula to these calls. Mom says X, then she says X+1, then she inverts the original claim, and says X is actually Y, *and* Y+1. At this point, because my attention has usually drifted, she will fill the silence by saying Y might also be Y minus one, to which I will say something crabby and she will apologize. At some point she will say, you sound Z (Z=annoyed, irritated, bothered) and I will say I'm sorry and she will say she's sorry to have made me Z, and we end the call.

My mother called. Said she had a colonoscopy on Tuesday so didn't remember if she had called me that night or not. I told her she had and we had a nice long talk. She said, "Aired out all our differences?" Later, she said if she were more modern she would text me instead of calling. I pointed out she had texted several times this week. She said, "Well, that's true."

My mother texted that she heard from Natty that Ben was an Illinois State Scholar. She texted him, "Congrats," then texted me asking if Ben had changed his number. I hollered to Ben to respond to Grandma's text. When she got his "Thank you," she called me. Started talking about the unusual snow they've had in New Mexico. She says snow isn't bad when it melts the next day but it gets bad in Albuquerque when it is too cold for the snow to melt. Again she mentioned Ben's Illinois State Scholar status. She said, she's pretty sure University of Illinois gets a notification of who is on that list as soon as it's published despite Ben and me saying we didn't think so.

My mother called. She sent a copy of her book, "Hanie Rides a Bike," to Gloria Steinem because it has such a positive feminist message. She had contacted Gloria's publisher who said contact her lawyer who said contact her assistant who said, "Send the book, Gloria will love it," and she did but never heard back. Not even a note saying she got it and that was a year ago. She hoped Gloria Steinem would be so impressed she would send it to Oprah Winfrey, who would feature it on her program. Thought my suggestion—send directly to Oprah—was a good one, but Oprah never responds to my mother's queries, not even when Oprah was just a Chicago TV host and my mom tried to interview her for Chicago Life Magazine. Agreed getting to Gayle King might work, "But even Gayle's too famous to reach now." Before this call I had not realized the titular "Hanie" was not the soft "Han" like Han Solo, but pronounced with the hard guttural "cha," like challah.

My mother called. She was stunned to learn McDonald's takes all their old fries and sends them to Kellogg's and that's how Pringles are made. Before I could stop myself, I said, "You couldn't possibly believe that." She wanted to know why not. I said, "If you even just for one second think about the mechanics." I said, "Every McDonald's shipping cooked food across the country?" I shouted, "Versus, the cost of Pringles just *buying* potatoes!" She said, "They do taste similar." I said, "They're both potatoes and oil. And salt." We never settled it to either of our satisfactions, although I said she might want to "Google it," which she did later and sent me a link from a message board where a writer named @sp55sagn said he worked for Pringles and confirmed it was true.

My brother's family got a new dog and started a text thread asking everyone to guess its name. I guessed "Rifle" because they are such vocal peaceniks it would be so obviously incorrect that it would be funny. My mother, who had guessed "Poopsie," texted that she didn't "get" Rifle. I texted that it was my guess in the Dog Name Game, and she texted again, "I still don't get it." I looked at my phone and shouted, "We were asked to guess the name of the dog and I guessed Rifle! What don't you get?" I was just talking to myself. One of them texted, "Rifle" would actually have been a good name because the dog was "rescued" from a "West Virginia" "puppy mill." Couldn't quite place the connection between that backstory and the name "Rifle," but it didn't seem productive at this point to respond, "I don't get it."

My mother called. She got into a car accident, a minor one, but before I could get any details, we had an argument about whether I already "heard about it." She thought that, in my initial response, the "What?" or "Whoa!" or whatever it was, she could detect I was faking. I assured her I had not heard about her being in a car accident, but she insisted I probably had from Emi. Talked about how at readings for her memoir, "The Who Behind Hanie," no one showed up other than her friends. She wondered if I experienced the same thing at my readings. I told her I don't have readings, don't publish books. I asked, Have *you* ever gone to a reading by someone you didn't know personally? She said, Not unless they're a well-known writer.

Lesson Eight: Think on your grudges often. Count them in the morning, display them on your walls, recite them at night.

Dreamt I saw a lion up the hill behind the mailbox where we are trying to grow the prairie grass. Sophie barked and ran to it and I was terrified, but the lion jumped over the fence and seemed afraid of Sophie.

I walked into a building on campus that I regularly cut through. I saw a new student and her father moving a rock to prop the door open. I said, "Hold it, hold it, hold it..." And dashed through the door and into an empty dorm room. The mattress was made of pine needles and I put my hand into the mound and pushed the needles around. A guy who worked in the building tried to sell me on the idea of buying a bigger food option. I said I don't really belong here and I could tell he already knew that and he was just toying with me.

Dreamt I was taking a shower and pulled a long hair clump out of the shower head, like what comes out of vacuum cleaner when the the hose gets clogged. Molly and I were walking along a block of homes that had a ton of junk in the front yard. Everyone was throwing out birdfeeders. A truck pulled up and said the homeowners owed him money. I went to a baseball game with Nick. Our seats were in a corridor winding around the top of the stadium and didn't even face the field. I said, "These seats are great!" Nick agreed but then he said, "Aren't we missing out on some of the fun back here?" I left my bike against a park bench in a city. I saw a homeless guy's feet sticking out of a blanket and I knew he would have to crawl over my bike to get out of his sleeping spot. I got on a train secure in the knowledge that like a horse, my Marrake$h bicycle would find her way home. Was in a saloon with a giant bar, with someone like Daryl although not exactly him. The bar was horseshoe shaped. I tried to use the tap to pour my own beer but I had no glass so when I pulled the handle, I ended up soaking my pants.

I was in front of a large building, and my mother was telling me that my father was coming to dinner. We went through a series of corridors because it was raining. I told her, I like walking the long way and I don't mind the rain. The buildings were packed tightly against each other, the walkways were narrow and dark. The rain filtered down through tubes between buildings. I looked in a mirror and had long hair and a ponytail which made me vaguely resemble Sarah Silverman, like a really ugly version of her. I was on an airplane with a bunch of rich people, and two of them were talking about a guy who had a ten million dollar suit but you couldn't tell how much it cost. I said, If I had a ten million dollar suit you would know it because I would have a giant price tag hanging off the sleeve that said, $10,000,000.

I was in a long line at a cafeteria at a college I had never been to before but was spending the night as part of some bike ride. I cut my way to the front and was handed a steak with part of it already eaten. I slammed my fist on the glass and said I had been on the ride and I was hungry. I walked out of the line through the outdoor commons area. I sat on a bench and started eating. A woman sitting behind me reached around and put her hand on my cheek as a joke and I put her finger in my mouth and kept chewing, which I thought was sort of gross but also bold. I thought, if Molly sees us I can make an excuse, point out this isn't really sexual at all, although it felt kind of sexy, chewing this woman's fingers.

Dreamt about a protest march. I was moving along in the crowd but really trying to get my bicycle—which I pushed and sometimes rode—to the place where I left my clothes. The bike had a flat tire and I rode on the rims of the wheels; no tubes, no tires. I was about to start working at Costello Labs again and I was arguing with my father about what shirt I should wear on my first day back. I was riding down a long canal and holding on to pillows, trying to keep them from getting wet as I jumped from one canal to the other. Madeleine was on a couch in the basement. I could see her from the top of the stairs; she was on one side and a baby deer was asleep on the other. Another animal, an eagle or another large bird, rested between them. I was trying to take a photo but didn't want to startle the deer with the flash. I was in a prison but I knew a mistake had been made with my paperwork and I was supposed to have been released, so I went to the prison guard and presented my case. Dreamt a fourth animal got through the window screen and it turned out to be a stuffed cat, an ugly one, constantly fighting with Beetee and Morty. Sophie, though she got along with the other two cats, viciously went after the new cat, causing it to hide under our bed.

Dreamt about a funeral service for my father, at which he was also present. It was RAGBRAI, the third or fourth day, and raining so I shivered under a tarp, still having a great time. I realized I have had no pie, no porkchop, no beer for days so I wasn't really doing RAGBRAI properly. I crossed a river in a small row boat along with a half-rabbit, half-woman creature. I was looking over old diary entries. There was a section break and I was thinking about a word I had used as a transition, wondering if it was the right one. I showed some foreign currency to Mike Strezewski, who took one of the bills and claimed it was his. He had a wallet full of cash from that country and called me arrogant. In the back of a church was a giant organ and it was not working. I put my finger into the slot to start it up and pulled a lever. It revved like a car motor but it didn't quite catch. Molly and I were trying to order a burger with extra fries and a woman said she could help us because she was the owner's mother. A mouse jumped on the table and landed on Molly's hamburger. She had taken the top bun off and held it so we could see the mouse curled up like a cat, sleeping right on the lettuce as if it were a cozy bed.

After a night at a carnival, Molly and the kids were talking about me going back to get the car. I was going to take the light rail to the parking lot, and Molly said, "Yeah, it's just like four blocks to where the train stop is." I was running to the lot and ended in an airport corridor. The road became an indoor passage, so I turned around. I saw the train was coming across the street on the other side of a chain-link fence. I waved to the conductor. The train had three levels and I was yelling, *I need to get on the train*. The conductor yelled, *You'll make it*. I got a seat next to a guy who looked like Dave Lucas. I thought it would be funny if I took a selfie with him and texted it to Dave and Joy and said, *Look I'm here with*

Dave. The guy was nice and cooperative but somehow I kept angling the phone wrong and I was only getting shots of the dog who lay across the seat in front of us.

Dreamt I had moved back to Spain. I was trying to figure out where my cot would go, looking out through the window at the pier we lived on. I was in Stu's bike shop which was in a mall; just a counter with a register and tools hanging off pegboard. I was wondering why he didn't set up a bike stand, make it look nice. Then I thought, Stu doesn't give a fuck, that's why. People were digging up plastic eggs that had been hidden in raised, indoor flower beds. Molly was saying she loved doing this because she had done it in France. When you found a plastic egg, which were plentiful and just lying on top of the dirt really, you had to open it and sniff the ball of clay inside. If it smelled like dung that was a good one and you took it home and cooked it. The person next to us opened one and sniffed it and said this was a good one. He let Molly sniff it and she agreed.

Dreamt Molly and I were in a hotel in bed and we were going to have sex, but the radiator was leaking on the floor, forming a giant puddle. Three shabbily dressed people walked in the room. I knew they were local street people who frequented the area but I was surprised they had gotten into our room. I was taking a writing workshop and turned in a ten page story. I saw the professor walking across the lobby and he mentioned he was thinking about workshopping my story in class. At some point I was massaging a fellow student and when I was rubbing her leg, she stopped me. I thought she was going to tell me to not massage near her private parts or that I should stop entirely. I was preparing to make my case, but she said she didn't want me to rub her knees because she had been injured. I kept going with the massage, this was through clothes, and then I kissed her neck and she got mad and stormed off. I knew it was wrong to do that but I needed to see what would happen, which I thought was a pretty good excuse if Molly ever found out about it.

Dreamt I was walking around a large industrial park where all the buildings looked the same. I was gutting a large alligator with a knife, peeling off the skin with one quick slice like it was a salmon. I met a woman from Instagram with a name I couldn't say because it had an underscore in it. She looked different from how she usually looked on the site. I was driving the Prius full of people over a wooden bridge which had many holes and ruts.

Underneath was water which we could see through the missing planks. Molly was saying that she would never try to drive over this bridge, and as she was saying so, I slipped and the car went underwater. Molly and Maggie stayed on the surface but as I climbed on the bridge with them I saw the car was gone. I was not panicked. I thought, I will simply commit suicide if the kids don't come up. Then Madeleine did come up and a few seconds later Ben did too. We five walked to the end of the bridge talking about how I had to get a new car and how I would have to tell Nick and Keith I had lost their books which were in the trunk. I didn't think we were making a big enough deal about how we had survived this accident. In the dream, I forced myself to cry.

Lesson Nine: A grudge is not a wristwatch, a grudge is a sundial. The grudge doesn't measure time, the grudge dictates time.

Rode Molly's bike to see Madeleine in the Hoogler Theater Company play. Locked bike to a tree and shuffled in to the middle school theater with a wave of grey haired patrons. Didn't buy a ticket and only nodded when the usher said, "Do you know how to find your seat?" Molly had seen it twice when I was doing RAGB-RAI and this was the final performance. Natty was somewhere in attendance with a bunch of her friends from a card-playing club, but I sat in the back alone. Having seen several other HTC productions, my plan was to listen to podcasts and only pay attention when Madeleine was on stage. The troupe had a strange tradition of starting shows by having a member of the cast, an Officious Fat Dude, come out and tell the audience how hard they had been working, then demanding a round of applause for the cast *before* the show started. Today he also read a list of the next couple shows they were planning and said everyone could support them by buying tickets for the 50/50 raffle during intermission. All of this had the effect of dampening any enthusiasm or excitement the audience may have felt.

The podcasts worked great except for the disorienting set-changes between scenes. In Hoogler, set changes are long: the crew stages each scene like they're arranging furniture in a home they just moved into, lots of questioning looks to one another, nudging tables, making slight adjustments to chairs and couches; often a crew member will step to the edge of the pit to take it all in before walking back to make more adjustments. While this was going on, I had perfectly audible podcast chatter in my head which I could not turn off because the light from my phone would have given me away.

During the intermission I headed to the concession stand in a hurry because my day-after-RAGBRAI-belly was yowling. The theater company was selling volunteer-baked goodies on small plates for a dollar each, and as I was handing over my buck, an older woman collapsed and hit the ground behind me. There was a sickening thud. I took my dollar back and asked the concession lady if I should call 911. She said we should get the actor playing the ship captain. "He's an EMT." I had my phone in my hand. I said, "Okay, but should I also call 911?" I pressed the nine and then the one, but it seemed like a lot of people were taking out their phones, so I hit delete and delete and put mine away. Then, because a crowd had formed around the fallen woman and there didn't seem to be anything to do, I handed over my dollar and took a plate with a cookie and a brownie. While I was eating, the Officious Fat Dude stepped to the edge of the ring and shouted, "Ladies and gentleman." I was sure he was going to ask everyone to step back and to give the woman on the ground some room, but he said, "Drawing for the 50/50 raffle will take place immediately before the second half so this is your last chance to...."

The parking lot wasn't very full, a couple dozen cars,

but there were two large red buses that said "Badger Tours, Madison," which explained why so many audience members were wearing lanyards with laminated badges. I ate my cookie and walked over to a guy smoking near the bus. I said, "Did you guys really come down from Madison?" He nodded. I said, "Just for this?" He nodded and turned away, but he kept a side-eye trained on me, so I said, "Ohh-kayyy..." He made a face and walked off.

I went back in the building. At some point the paramedics had come and taken the woman out on a stretcher. I found Natty who was standing in the lobby with a group of her friends. One of them had painted eyebrows arched so severely she looked like the Hamburglar. Another friend said, "Does anyone know anything about the woman who fell?"

I said, "I saw her fall. What do you want to know?"

I assumed she wanted to know if the fall looked serious or how the woman was doing, but Natty's friend asked, "Is she local or part of the tour group?"

I didn't know the answer, but I said, "Local. No laminated badge." I was surprised by my reasoning and my confidence.

I took my seat in the back of the balcony. Officious Fat Dude came out before the curtain went up just in case

anyone had any lingering good will toward the show.
He clutched a handheld wireless mic and waited for us
to quiet down so he could reach into his hat and pull a
ticket. The winner of the 50/50 hooted for joy when her
name was called, a local, and she took her 84 dollars and
didn't donate it back.

Madeleine sang Western People Funny and was won-
derful, but I do sort of wonder how much longer anyone is going to be performing this musical. When she
was done I put the earbuds back in. Because I was one
day post RAGBRAI, I drifted off and was awoken by the
sound of my own snoring, which I could hear over the
podcast. I had woken in the middle of some long dance
number and it occurred to me I had no idea what was
being danced about or what the narrative was at all. It
seemed to be be about the American civil war which was
baffling to me since I thought the musical was set in
Bangkok.

After the show I hugged Madeleine in the Kiss and
Cry, said goodbye to Natty and her gang, unlocked Molly's bike and started riding home listening to music: The
Ramones and The Babies. I almost never listen to music
when I ride, but I was in such a good mood I was kind
of more dancing than pedaling. At some point I heard
frenzied honking from a van and when I turned back

I saw it was Sam who had been on RAGBRAI too. He posted something on Facebook about seeing me ride my bike just one day after RAGBRAI, and Hawk Yeah Sharon commented that she couldn't believe I wasn't taking a break. I answered I was on a different bike, that I didn't need a break, but I had given my bike one.

Lesson Ten: There are eight kinds of terrain in which a grudge can thrive.

1)Swamp.

I told Finn Lee I was jealous his office had a couch in it. At some point my reading glasses fell out of my pocket, but I didn't see it happen and wouldn't realize it until I was already across campus at the seminar. Because of the position of the couch and the window—which had blinds that were closed—I accused Finn of being able to lie on the couch to look at porn. I was joking, but Finn said he never looked at porn in his office because he thought the library administrators could check his computer. He said, "It would have to be something library related. Or art."

I said, "Charlotte1996 does some interesting things. She's kind of a genius to begin with, but some of her videos are definitely art." I told him about one I had seen, just her solo on a bed, and as she's getting into it, the shot cuts to what she was looking at: "A point of view shot, to the ceiling lamp over her bed. One of those breast-shaped dome lamps." The video makes clear that the shape of the lamp is arousing to her. The cinematographer does a special effect where the lamp becomes two breasts in her imagination. They even jiggle a little on the ceiling. I compared it to the classic Japanese crime film "In the Realm of the Senses," which also uses "non-simulated sex," but Finn wasn't a big movie guy and didn't know the Japanese movie.

He asked, "What's the other one called, the one with Charlotte1996?"

I said, "Bored Girl Masturbates to Ceiling Titty."

2) *Canyons.*

We four did the crossword mini together. Went well until we hit a snag on "old expression." Molly said some word no one ever heard of so we ignored her, but we eventually figured out the answer was "adage" and what Molly had been saying was *ah-dodge*, as if it were a French word. When Ben called her on it, she insisted that's how people say it in English too, and not *add-ij* which we were saying.

Ben went back into the deBasement and I tried to read the opening section from the Denmark story out loud to Molly and Madeleine. Molly interrupted immediately to say, "Buddha, she said Buddha," then "That's not true, we did not say that." Then, "And she was fat! The conductor was fatter than dad!" and finally I got angry, "You have interrupted every single sentence!" Madeleine shut down when I started yelling, asked me what it was like to be an "asshole."

Factoring in my neediness to be told "good job" with this outcome and all of it taking place in about 20-40 seconds, it may have been my least successful minute on Earth.

3) Forest.

I sat next to Juli during my mom's bat mitzvah slash 76th birthday service. Whispered about the latest with Robert, our cats, lots of stuff. I told her I took her last edible awhile ago and she said she prefers chocolate bars because they're more potent and taste better. She took out a chocolate bar from her purse and broke off a piece. "You want some?" I took it and held it for a moment. I had been drinking all day, one at the airport, two on the plane, but paced out, low level, no buzz. I could just tell Molly to drive in case it "came on" while we were in the car. I decided to only eat half, did, and then ended up eating the rest of it. The chocolate was chewy and I didn't taste the marijuana much but I did start to feel a little floaty. I said, "It's too early to feel anything, right?"

Juli said, "It's a Three Musketeers. I bought it in a gas station."

I said "It's stale."

She said, "I don't think they sell a lot of them."

4) Glacier.

Got an email from Beau Wilder that he liked Prompt & Product for Bellwa Fiction Journal but wanted me to publish it as an essay instead of fiction. Said he could "make a case for that." Reread essay with the idea that it would be published and it made me proud, which always happens when someone says something nice about something I wrote. Read email to Molly and realized when Beau wrote, "I can make a case for publishing" he wasn't saying "as nonfiction," he was saying publish it at all. In fact reading it closer, he wrote "the students rejected it but they can't do it," and I thought "it" meant he would not let them reject my story, but now I saw he meant reject without him knowing, which is why he had contacted me, to tell me they were rejecting it.

I called Wilder. I said, "When I first saw your email I

thought you were taking Prompt & Product but when I reread it I thought you were *not* taking it. Which is it?"

Not taking it. He claimed to love the story but the undergrads he works with wouldn't publish anything by a middle-aged man talking about jerking off. He assured me, "I do have final say but I have to work with them so I don't think I can do much."

I said, "We have different ideas about what 'final say' means."

He asked about other stories and I lied and said I have three of them from Book of Grudges already placed, then correct it and say, "Two since you're not taking Prompt & Product." But I actually only have one, so when he asked where, I said Santa Monica Review, which is true, and then had to pause because I couldn't think of a place to lie about, but managed to say, Grammar Train.

He said, "Oh wow. That's a good one. Congrats."

5) Marshes.

Watched a series of documentaries about pillow humping. One is called, "Red-Hair Girl Humps a Pillow" and another is, "Brunette-Hair Girl Humps a Pillow." Both women have slightly different techniques, not just the humping but also camera angles and pacing, but I discover on a repeat viewing, both-hair-girls are the same person. Part of what gives it away is a distinctive pillow—not the the pillow being humped but a throw pillow leaning against the headboard—and that her glasses are the same. As the brunette-hair girl, her foot hits the blinds once and it makes a distracting crackling sound.

There was also, "Blonde-Hair Girl Humps a Pillow" but I already had my hands full with the first two.

6) *Oasis.*

While having a beer in Rockford with Molly, I talk about an idea I have for a Podcast called *Straight No Chaser.* She asks what it will be about and I say, I don't know, I just have the name. I say, "But it's good, right? Wouldn't you listen to a Podcast called *Straight, No Chaser?*"

She considers it for a moment. Then says, "I don't know where my Airpods are."

When we go to bed that night I make about as sweet an overture as I can but she declines. "Is that why you wanted to have dinner out? Just so we can do that?"

"Of course not," I say. But then after she's asleep I think of a better answer: So what?

7) *Gravel.*

Went to Mel's Market just before it opens as directed by Corrine. Helped set up the booth—we were between the Hoogler County Chamber of Commerce and Timmy B's Local Honey. It was pretty clear Corrine could handle it all herself; she was probably confused when I volunteered but felt obligated to give me a shift.

A woman came up and looked at the rainbow t-shirts and eyed me suspiciously. I gave her a sticker and a pamphlet and explained that all proceeds were going to help LGBTQ youth in the community. She warmed up after that and we shook hands. She said, "I'm the only out trans woman in Hoogler County," which was probably true.

I said, "I'm Dan."

She leaned in and whispered into my ear. She had cigarette and coffee breath, like a math teacher. She said, "It's always unsettling for me to meet a Dan." She told me I have her dead name.

I bet it is unsettling. I bet for her, meeting a "Dan" must be like observing a row of cars after changing lanes in a traffic jam, watching its progress. I bet when it's me, when Dan Libman is the Dan with your dead name, you probably feel pretty good about your decision to change lanes.

When she left, Corrine said, "It's a real honor to be told someone's dead name."

I said, "I know."

Tug and Jaycee Halper came by and took a polite but extremely quick glance at the rainbow mugs. I felt some affection for them because I had been working on the story about The Greens, and just as I was about to say hello, a guy I recognized as another volunteer came up and hugged Jaycee. They started laughing and talking about the current summer of JoyRiding out at the The Greens.

I was stunned. Of course they were doing it again this year, but no one had reached out to me, despite Susanna perpetually struggling to find volunteers. I felt left out, hurt. It also made me feel paranoid, a word no one had used to describe being excluded during our sensitivity training on campus.

8) *Tundra.*

Finished my first pass on Snow Day Sunday and I understand it has a long way to go but I also understand I might be getting there. Removed all the references to Charlotte1996 and Mink Foxx but think I will leave in the part about the nude photo of me. I think the story is about a bad artist finding inspiration and then not being able to meet the moment. Maybe I can submit the story as a nonfiction essay instead of fiction. Maybe I should be doing that for all of them.

Checked the mail and found our replacement credit card for the one the one we lost. Molly was in the bathroom, and I told her I would go online and update all our subscription accounts: Amazon and Netflix and Home Box Office Maximum and Criterion and Spoterfy mm-hmm (I always say it like Slingblade) and PayPal and the Illinois Tollway iPass and her Mud Water and Nuts Dot Com and New York Times (both news *and* games subscriptions) and Washington Post and Major League Baseball Audio and all the other companies that have sent kind notes over the past ten days wondering why my payments weren't being processed.

I was pretty glum, dreading all the tedious online work ahead for me, but Molly was relieved. She said, "At last things are normal again!" Then she held a small tea pot to her face and poured water in one of her nostrils and let it drip out the other nostril into the sink.

Lesson Eleven: A worthwhile grudge will be taken up by the entire village.

The Tenured and Tenure-Track Faculty, their gossamer souls infused with peace, meet once a week to discuss English Department doin's. An instructor gets to sit on the council because our union bargained for it. Generally, I am that instructor by virtue of the fact that no one else wants to give up their Wednesday lunch hour. It's easier to schedule the Professorial Tenured and Tenure-Track faculty since they teach two classes in the fall semester and two in the spring, whereas we instructors teach four classes in the fall and then four more classes in spring.

Today, the male Doctor Mercy-Leushius—Doctor Theodore Mercy-Leushius—brought donuts and put them in the center of the conference table to much excited finger-waving from the assembled doctors. He said, "I wish I thought to bring napkins," and indeed the few doctors who took donuts, Doctor Bustello Lochboisdale, Doctor Simchat Cwningen closing her Chrome book to reach over, and I think Doctor Ghislaine Ashtonschriek, all held their donuts aloft in outstretched arms to avoid spilling crumbs on their earthly vessels. They ate their donuts and scanned the copy of last week's minutes.

Doctor David Welsh-Carrot walked in late and was told immediately about the donut situation.

"Theodore brought donuts," Inez Mercy-Leushius, the female Doctor Mercy-Leushius, said. Doctor Welsh-Carrot smacked his lips exaggeratedly which made us all laugh, and after plucking a pink frosted from the Dunkin box, surveyed the table.

Doctor Inez Mercy-Leushius said, "No napkins." She was married to Doctor Theodore Mercy-Leushius, and also our presumptive next chair. The chair search committee, which I also sit on as instructor Faculty representative, had been empaneled, and while we had not yet made a recommendation, Doctor Mercy-Leushius was our only candidate and had been training under the current Acting Chair, Doctor Pete Smith.

The male Doctor Mercy-Leushius again said, "I wish I had thought to bring napkins."

I thought he was just trying to remind us he was the one who brought the donuts in the first place since Doctor Welsh-Carrot hadn't thanked him, but Doctor Welsh-Carrot only assured him the lack of napkins wasn't an issue for him. In fact, "not a jot" was the phrase he used to quantify how little it mattered.

"I believe it's Simchat's turn to keep the minutes," acting chair Doctor Smith said, and Doctor Cwningen re-opened her laptop with a pained expression which made us all chuckle.

I looked out the window while the doctors scanned the minutes and chewed donuts and brushed the crumbs on to the floor for the janitorial staff

Doctor Quentin Palfreyman said, "Let me know when you're ready to vote on the minutes."

Normally this would be the job of Doctor Smith, Acting Chair, but today was the day the council took up the performance review of departmental leadership including Doctor Smith, so Doctor Palfreyman was acting in the role of Acting Chair for the meeting.

Doctor Palfreyman, who was gaunt and sallow like a scarecrow, had not taken a donut but had brought his own napkin, which he unfolded on the table in front of him, creating a makeshift placemat. On the floor beside him was a double bagged brown grocery sack from which he began pulling a series of Tupperware and freezer bags. From one, he took a single grape, examined it like he was wearing a jeweler's loupe, then popped it in his mouth. After chewing for a moment, he reached into the baggie for another grape. Doctor Palfreyman had written the minutes so was the only doctor not perusing last week's notes. (Nota bene: perusing means to "read carefully and thoroughly," which is the opposite of what you think it means.) I was also not reading the minutes because I was not given a copy, an oversight for which Doctor Smith apologized, just as he has apologized every week since assumin' actin' chairship, since he never brought a copy for me, presumably because I was just the instructor rep. My only recourse is to abstain from voting on motions, a mild protest on the grounds that I haven't been allowed to read them.

Doctor Cwningen took issue with a lack of semi-colon in one of the items, in fact it was the item about how last week they had approved the previous week's minutes, and Doctor Welsh-Carrot assured us the phrase contained meaning without the "pernicious mark" but that he "took her point" and would second the motion. A vote was taken: nine yea votes, one abstention, the typo would be fixed.

Doctor Lochboisdale noted the margins were out of alignment on one item and Doctor Palfreyman, mouth full of corn chip, agreed to fix the matter without taking it to vote. He had now removed a loaf of bread from the bag—not a slice of bread, but an entire loaf—separated two slices, and packed the rest of the bread back into the grocery sack. He then took out two convenience store mayonnaise packets and squirted mayonnaise on one slice of bread, and the second pack of mayonnaise on the other, spreading the mayonnaise with a plastic knife. He removed, from one of the opaque Tupperware, two slices of deli meat, their sheens glinting under the fluorescent lights, placed one slice of turkey on each piece of mayonnaise'd bread, then pressed them together. Like a nervous swimmer cautiously testing the waters of a new pool, he examined his work closely, then took a small bite.

While this was happening, Doctor Smith asked if there were any other changes to the minutes, and there being none, took a vote on their adoption, and the motion passed, nine yeas to one abstention.

Before we did the performance reviews, Doctor Smith said we had to discuss "the letter." He then passed out copies of the final draft for everyone to read, since we would all need to sign.

Doctor Smith said, "And sorry Dan, ha ha, I forgot to make a copy for you."

Doctor Gora Addala-Shukhgel'meer said, "He can read mine," and slid the paper across the table to me. She was spearheading this campaign and she wanted all of us to sign it, even me, since that would make us look more resolved.

We the undersigned, the full members of the English Department Council, are outraged by the comments from the

Chair of the Bureau of Gender and Sexuality directed toward Dr. Addala-Shukhgel'meer, Ph.D., synecdochic member of the full English Department Council, on the matter of the adoption of the Gender Neutral Facility on the second floor of Beeswing Hall….

I was distracted by a steady *thuk thuk thuk* coming from the end of the table. Doctor Palfreyman had a vanilla Greek yogurt container tipped up to his face, and was using a spoon to scrape the sides and bottom. Satisfied he had mined the last ounce of yogurt, he put the spoon in his mouth and grunted a joyless, "mm."

This draft of the letter was the next chapter in the semester long saga over the Gender Neutral Bathroom, proposed by The Bureau of Gender and Sexuality. The English Department Council had been asked to respond to the initial proposal, for which everyone had been overwhelmingly in favor. The problem came from the doctors trying trying to outdo each other in being supportive. Doctor Ashtonschriek had suggested making available warm towels to users of the gender neutral facility. Doctor Lochboisdale advocated for a hospitality basket by the sinks which might contain items such as breath mints and dental floss, as well as pamphlets from all the wellness, counseling, and brave/safe spaces on campus.

Doctor Addala-Shukhgel'meer, in an attempt to top them all, had voiced the opinion that the proposal to convert a single Female Faculty Bathroom, did not go far enough. She thought the Male Faculty Bathroom should also be converted. And though Doctor Addala-Shukhgel'meer had several degrees in applied linguistics and had written pioneering papers on Information Transference, she was a surprisingly horrible communicator. She used the word "unfair" to describe the conversion of the Female Faculty Bathroom, and just assumed everyone would understand the part about also wanting the Male Faculty Bathroom converted.

The Chair of the Bureau of Gender and Sexuality had taken offense. She drafted her own response letter. "Just as supporters of Jim Crow eventually came to accept bathrooms shared by all races, I am confident certain members of the English Department will come around to the idea of Gender Equality here in Beeswing Hall."

The letter we were composing in response to The Bureau's response to our response to their proposal, expressed multi-syllabic pique at the comparison, contained acrobatic rhetoric, and so many commas it would have made Proust blush. *We write this letter to wrestle back the honor, not just of our comrade, but of all of us, of anyone who cares about the humanities!* As I skimmed my copy, I could see the letter never explicitly said the thing driving Doctor Addala-Shukhgel'meer, which is that she wanted an apology for being likened to a segregationist.

Several objections on wording and punctuation were voiced, although no one pointed out the utter lack of clarity, and ultimately the Council decided to let Doctor Addala-Shukhgel'meer write an additional draft: motion to sign letter tabled until next week went forward with ten yeas, even me, just to move things along.

Doctor Palfreyman said we needed to begin the performance reviews anyway, and asked Doctor Smith to step outside. Doctor Smith made a few jokes about his fate being in our hands, at which we all chuckled, except for Doctor Welsh-Carrot who threw his head back and roared at such delicious bons mots.

While Doctor Palfreyman shook an aerosol can of Ready Whip and drew a whooshing circle of whipped cream on top of a single serving cup of Ben and Jerry's ice cream wrapped in an ice pack with rubber bands, the doctors began muttering about Doctor Smith's performance. There was general agreement that Doctor Smith's performance was below expectations (Doctor Ashtonschriek's words), and that his handling of a certain, ahem, personnel issue had been subpar (Doctor Lochboisdale's words and pointed throat clearing,) and that he was on the whole a super shitty administrator (my paraphrase). Nevertheless, we were still going to gush and give him the highest possible rating. They began offering flowery phrases to word our mendacious encomium (my phrase, which I didn't say but jotted down for later).

"While his academic faculties remain largely intact," Doctor Ashtonschriek said slowly, allowing Doctor Cwningen time to type it out on her Chromebook. "His approach to institutional organization allows... room for growth."

Doctor Welsh-Carrot chuckled ruefully.

In the spirit of jocularity, Doctor Palfreyman observed, "We could list Pete's not having pursued the Chair as a strength."

I said, "That's actually not nothing."

What I meant was, by stepping back, Doctor Smith removed the possibility of a departmental rift between backers of his candidacy and people who wanted Doctor Inez Mercy-Leushius. As Acting Chair, he might even have had an edge over her, though clearly the inferior choice. Doctor Inez Mercy-Leushius was clear eyed, organized, and—rare for our department—had a warm personality. By sparing the department having to choose, Doctor Smith had done us a mitzvah. That was what I meant, but I was not allowed to explain, because Doctor Palfreyman immediately announced, "I was just being sardonic," then he turned to me and added, "which means sarcastic."

It was about this time that Doctor Richard May came in. He explained his lateness by telling us he had been locked in his garage and had required a mechanic with a crowbar to extricate him. As soon as he sat down, Doctor Palfreyman told him we were actually just about to do his review. He was excused, but could he send Doctor Smith back?

During the transition, when Richard left and we waited for Doctor Smith to return, I told the doctors I had to meet my class in twenty minutes, but since we were in computer lab today I would quickly post a message on Blackboard with the assignment and have them start without me. Doctor Palfreyman offered his assurance that my part of the meeting would not take long. "In fact," he said, "Why don't you give us the instructor input on Doctor May right now."

I said the instructors were uniformly happy with Richard's leadership and we would give him the highest rating possible. Doctor Cwningen tapped out a few key strokes on her Chromebook.

I said, "I have collected comments from the instructors," and held up my paper. "Just some specific things they appreciate about the support we receive from Richard." I told the doctors I would be happy to read the comments into the record, but I would also leave the paper for them.

Doctor Palfreyman said, "Neither will be necessary and the instructor input has been noted."

Doctor Cwningen hit one keystroke on the number pad of her Chromebook and nodded a confirmation.

Doctor Palfreyman then thanked me for coming in and apologized for keeping me so long. The doctors all smiled kindly at me as I gathered my things and went off to teach my class.

Lesson Twelve: Appear the most mollified when at your bitterest, be conciliatory while your grudge festers.

Genghis Kahn was the first Mongol emperor, Kublai Kahn was the Yuan emperor, and Madeleine Kahn was in Blazing Saddles. Kubla Kahn is a poem by Coleridge; Kukla, Fran and Ollie was a television show.

Spare Time Bar in the bowling alley was packed tonight, twelve teams. B2 in classic formation: Daryl at the corner of the bar, Jack to his right, me to his left. Ben and Noel both came with me this evening and sat to the left of me. Had a new bartender named Nikki; she had worked at some bar in Rockford and she and Daryl seemed to know each other. Who has more bones, a full grown adult or a baby? We five have to really talk it out before answering but guessed right. Could only name two of the four Who Wants To Be A Millionaire hosts. B2 was up near the top when Matt announced scores before betting on the final question. We pulled Ben's Sun Tzu maneuver *and* were in the allowable range for the adding question: Number of Heisman trophy winners from Michigan (Daryl could actually name them), plus number of "drummers drumming," plus number of U.S. cities beginning with S in the list of 20 most populated, plus number of studio Pearl Jam albums. Jack was so confident he signaled for a Victory Round even before The Moops or Smarty Pants settled their second place tie breaker. Nikki was pleased we won and declared herself our "lucky charm," unaware that we regularly do well. She handed out the tabs and in my customer ID field she had typed, "Daryl's Friend." Everyone laughed but it didn't bother me at all; I like being Daryl's friend and am fine being known for that. When Nikki gave my credit card back she said, "Daniel. I'll remember next time, Daniel."

Only four teams tonight, reduced to three when the ringer from Underachievers had to leave early. Jack also MIA so we were just Ben, Noel, Daryl and me. Felt more lively than usual despite trivia's sparse crowd because the bowling lanes were packed. We could hear the pins crashing steadily and Matt kept turning his mic louder until the feedback squealed. Eighteenth century earl, John Montagu is better known as what? How many quarterbacks have won super bowls with two different teams? Came in third behind Moops and Hawk Yeah. Didn't get food but bought a three dollar Snickers from kids on the wrestling team. One of the women in Smarty Pants came up to me and said, "I won't be seeing you again because I'm moving to Montana." She was a little emotional to be saying goodbye but we don't even know each other's names.

Arrange in order from highest to lowest: Number of feet in the Chrysler building, year Galileo died, highest number of running yards ever in a single football game, and the weight of a cubed foot of silver. No Nikki tonight, a new bartender being trained by surly Blake. Daryl, Jack and I agreed it was unbecoming for men in their fifties to be talking about young women, but the new bartender, we had to at least acknowledge, was very attractive. Jack said he has no right to judge the looks of anyone and described himself as "a four." I thought that was low, that he was at least a six, maybe even a seven because he was in shape, had a "wholesome look," and went to his job in a firefighter's class A dress uniform. Because I had answered the question about People Magazine's Sexiest Man Alive I didn't want to also argue that Jack was good looking. I did venture that if Jack was a four, then I was at best a two, "Maybe 2.5 depending on the lighting." Daryl stayed quiet. He offered no opinions about how either one of us looked. Or his own looks. Or the young bartender's.

Set out for bowling alley with Ben and Noel and Molly. No trivia tonight because it's Halloween, but we went anyway to check the Football Pick-Em standings. Molly wanted a night without her mom and Spanky, although she felt guilty and we ended up talking about them a lot. The bowling alley did not yet have last week's results posted despite it being Wednesday, so we went to Geezer's for dinner even though Molly said she preferred the bowling alley food, which was confusing to those of us who eat it regularly. Our waitress was dressed as a sexy cat and said she was impressed I could "even drink" a

Dogfish Head 120. Because of that I ordered a second one and because of *that* I'm hazy on most of the night.

Nikki's boyfriend, Nick, has started coming Wednesday nights. He usually sits at the far end of the bar by himself. I asked tonight, and Nikki does not think it's weird they both have the same name. I knew an answer about Trotsky but couldn't remember his name. Daryl and Jack guessed Lenin and Marx. I said, "Keep going." They just looked at me. I said, "Took a pickaxe through the head in Mexico," which triggered Daryl to say Trotsky just in time because the only other thing I could have added was, "Jewish," which would not have helped them. Our glasses were emptier than usual because Nikki and Nick stepped out the side door several times during the game. He has delicate features and is a foot shorter than she is, and in the window we could could see her silhouette bobbing like a duck, taking hits off his vape pen. When Nikki returned she filled our pint glasses and gave us free apple pie shots in plastic cups.

Ben and I picked up Noel and drove to the bowling alley. Daryl and Jack already there. Looked at Football Pick-Em standings. Everyone at the bar was buzzing because the high school football team got caught in some bizarre hazing ritual involving Oreo cookies. It's going to be a story on the *teevee* news and a camera crew had been in the bar to get "reaction." The details are murky and gross and folks in the bowling alley were calling it "cookiegate." I kept saying "double stuffghazi" but it didn't catch on. Tied for third at the half but had a tremendous run, named all six hosts of the Tonight Show, where the Azores are, and which element is listed as PB on the periodic table. Pulled Ben's Sun Tzu maneuver which caused the other teams to bet incorrectly at the final question. Ended up in second place and got another 15 dollar gift card to the bowling alley to add to our pile.

Ben filled out our Football Pick-Em sheets. Nikki brought Daryl his Corona and my Guinness. Tonight I ordered the "veggie" wrap, assuming it would be light, but it was not. What three words make up the the portmanteau: *Tribeca*? Apparently Ben and Daryl have been trolling on a thread in the unofficial town Facebook group where one of the football moms called the cookie hazing incident, "Good clean fun." Good and fun are debatable, but if the rumors are true about where they put those cookies, "clean" it was not. Another mom wrote that unless you had a son on the football team you should, "not even have an opinion!" Dead silence when Matt announced our third victory in a row. We had to wait awhile for the victory round because Nikki and Nick were vaping outside. I took the remaining half of the veggie wrap for Molly, but then I ate it while driving home.

Tonight we did badly in the first half but got lucky when the middle question was about World War I. Between the four of us we've listened to Dan Carlin's Blueprint for Armageddon six times. Managed second place by guessing whose motto was, "Leave the driving to us," then Sun Tzu'ing the field. Nikki's boyfriend played by himself under the team name, "Nick." He answered a few questions then lost interest and stood outside the side door vaping with Nikki. We griped about our beers not being refilled. Team Nick ended up with three points, which Matt announced with the rest of scores. Everyone clapped politely. B2 scored 142, losing to the Moops with 146.

Just Daryl and me for awhile tonight, then Ben, Madeleine, and Noel showed up. Ben filled out our Football Pick-Em sheets, Noel filled out his. Next week I need to pick up the turkey in Rockford around the same time my mother will arrive at the bus depot. I kept saying, "I'm going to have to go to Rockford to pick up that difficult old bird… and the turkey." The joke didn't work but the kids tried to help. I kept getting mixed up, saying, "Pick up that old bird and my mother." Finally Madeleine declared it, "Too contrived," and refused to hear it anymore. What does ZIP of zip code stand for? Who starred in Calamity Jane? Guinness keg blew out and I complained about it to Matt when I handed him an answer slip. He said he hadn't gotten the free Sprite he's entitled to as the "Trivia Jockey." We were so far in the lead at the final question we didn't bother Sun Tzu'ing and still won. After the Victory Round, Nikki gave us free drink chips. She asked Ben, "How long until you're 21?" Ben said, "A few months." Nikki slid him a drink chip. She said, "Hold on to this, I want to buy your first beer." I got a little misty. On the way home we talked about how sweet Nikki is and how we just wished she was better at tending bar.

Tonight the bar was out of Daryl's first, second and third choice beers. Nikki said the woman who orders beer has been on vacation. I've been drinking Pabst which I have to call PBR or Nikki says they don't have it. Taylor came with Daryl and got an elaborate tropical drink because for some reason she told Nikki, "Surprise me." It had an umbrella and a pineapple, which, I had to admit, was surprising. Which book did Mark Twain publish first: Tom Sawyer, Connecticut Yankee, or Huck Finn? We guessed Connecticut Yankee but should have gone with Tom Sawyer because I knew it had come before Huck Finn so the odds were 50/50 instead of one in three, plus it was the correct answer. Put on steam when others flailed and we were up by 19 points at the final question which we got wrong but had only bet two points. Team Shaken Bacon got it right, bet a baffling 15 points instead of the full 20 and came in second even though they could have beaten us. Matt scolded them for dumb betting and they admitted they were trying to protect second place. Matt was genuinely upset by this and spent some time at their table going over the numbers.

Ben and I ordered chicken drummies this time. Daryl got a BLT. Nikki handed out engagement announcements which included a poem, the gist of which was that we shouldn't feel obligated, but if we wanted to give her and Nick a present, they could "use some money." Daryl said we should give them the bowling alley gift cards we keep winning and not using. Name the volcano that destroyed Pompei. What does AARP stands for? All teams contending at the final question, (except team "Nick," nine points on the night), but because we bet smart and Sun Tzu'd the field, we earned a Victory Round.

Nikki out and surly Blake was our bartender. He's a better bartender than Nikki but doesn't root for us. I always think he'll be happy to see me because Molly was his teacher at DeKalb State and he likes her, but he grew up here so lots of his customers are his former teachers. Daryl and Jack arrived together, and I drank nitro Guinness from cans all night. Add the number of original members of Menudo, the number of James Bond films with Sean Connery, the number of seats in the house of representatives belonging to New York state, plus the number of Major League Baseball players inducted into the Hall of Fame on the first ballot. Noel asked Blake to change channels to a soccer game and he did, but not happily. What do you call music stolen and released illegally? I remembered that when Rerun snuck a reel to reel tape machine into the Doobie Brothers concert it was called "bootlegging," which was correct. Matt said all the other teams guessed "pirated."

Nikki was gone on her honeymoon and tonight's trainee bartender looked like she was in high school.

Surly Blake was training her and she seemed nervous. Who is older, Idris Elba, Will Farrell, or some guy we've never heard of? Guess the other guy and he turns out to be youngest. Doesn't get much better from there. Name either one of the two women on the AFI list of "Top 50 Film Heroes." I thought it would be someone like Norma Rae and not Wonder Woman because that's too new. Daryl suggested Princess Leia which seemed like a great choice and we went with it but the correct answer was either Clarise Starling or Ripley from Alien. Which famous Shakespeare play begins with a sea storm? Daryl disagreed with me because he thought The Tempest wasn't "famous" like Hamlet or Romeo and Juliet. I argued it was just a poorly worded question because all Shakespeare's plays are famous. I tried to pull the Sun Tzu maneuver but Matt said those three sneaky points wouldn't even put us in the top five tonight. The trainee bartender handed us our tabs. In the customer ID field for Daryl she put, "Trivia Beard." For me she had typed, "Trivia Old."

Nikki was back tonight. She claimed she can only work one night a week and chose Wednesdays because of us. We knew where the Kamchatka Peninsula was, were pretty sure who did the voice for Lil Penny in the

Nike ads, and got a true/false wrong about American Pie being the name of plane Buddy Holly died in. Has a supreme court justice ever been impeached? I argued no, reasoning that if it had ever happened, I would have heard about it. This turned out to be bad logic because it did happen, apparently in 1805, the news just had not reached me yet. We finished off the podium and Daryl said it was because I have been bringing the wrong pen. I lost the lucky pen a few weeks ago and have been handing him a lookalike hoping he wouldn't notice.

Nikki hadn't saved our corner this evening so we sat halfway down the bar across from the taps but in the usual arrangement: Daryl in the middle, Jack to his right, me to his left. Ordered a chicken sandwich which was shockingly good: thick chicken patty, fresh tomato, brioche bun. Something I could regularly order. What color is 13 on a roulette table? Which is the first Rolling Stones album to use the lips and tongue logo? Name three of the four NBA teams to have back to back championships in the last 25 years. Thought H. P. Lovecraft had probably invented zombies but because the question was about biting, we went with vampires and got it wrong. Missed only one digit on the first six digits of pi. Wanted to tell Matt it was amazing we got as many as we did without Noel or Ben, but they don't give points for that. Who did Tom Sawyer live with? Daryl said Aunt Sally and I thought Aunt Polly. Jack remembered Aunt Becky but only after I had already turned in our sheet. Fortunately, because we weren't confident, I had just written, "His aunt," and Matt gave it to us. That made Daryl *un*happy because Matt had not given us credit for "Put a Ring on It" when the answer was "Single Ladies." Add the numbers associated with a quinceañera, the number of Sopranos seasons, the total of the first eight prime numbers, and the number of letters in the Cyrillic alphabet, which is the only one we didn't know so we came up with a number outside the range. Scored so low Sun Tzu'ing was no help. Matt said, "B2 is in a rut!" The car was covered in snow and had to be brushed and scraped before I could drive home.

Ordered the chicken sandwich but what came out tonight was horrible; the bowling alley is back to the thin, grocery store patties and tasteless tomatoes. I ate it but it made me angry. Got United States correct when asked which country hosted the 1996 Olympics. Matt said most teams put Atlanta and he gave them credit, even though Atlanta is not a country. Matt noticed Daryl was fuming so he told us he had given us "Green Arrow" when the name of the show is actually "Arrow." He also gave credit to teams who had answered, "Roman Empire," for the question, "When Francis II abdicated his throne in 1806, he was the last emperor of what empire?" The correct answer was, "Holy Roman Empire." This didn't help us because we put "Ottoman," which we had also misspelled.

Tonight, when Nikki asked if I wanted a menu, I said, "I'm not eating here anymore to protest the change in the chicken sandwich." She said, "Don't you dare do that to me," which was not a response I was prepared for. She gave Daryl, Jack and me each a sample of of a winter beer from Sam Adams. We didn't like it. Jack said, "It tastes like cider." Nikki said, "That's what was in the tap before." Later she told us apropos of almost nothing that she has a pair of zebra-fur handcuffs at home but they are too large for Nick's wrists. How many directing Oscars did Alfred Hitchcock win in total? We were in fifth place at the half but only missed one after that and bounced into first place for the final question about remakes of the film, A Star is Born. We bet zero but got our three sneaky Sun Tzu points and won. Molly already asleep when I got back so headed into the deBasement. People would be surprised if they knew how often trivia champs end up spending victory nights alone watching TV.

Had to sweep melt water out of the garage before Ben and I headed out to trivia. Daryl was already there. Surly Blake behind the bar, and when he handed me the menu I told him the story of the chicken sandwich and my protest. He said he would look into it. I have told him before and that's what he always says. B2 would have ended up in third but we tied for first with Smarty Pants via the Sun Tzu trick. Our first place runoff question was, "How many votes did Al Gore lose by in 2000?" Ben knew the answer was low and guessed 376. Smarty Pants guessed 6000. The answer was 576. I pointed out Ben was really only off by two in one digit, but he honorably said he had been wrong by 200. The main Smarty Pant said, "I thought we beat you but I guess I misheard the score before the final bet." She had a sweet smile and a sweater that said, "Grace." She walked over to Matt and flashed a napkin full of calculations. Before I could get over to Matt's table, he was already explaining it. "They got three bonus points for sharing the clue on Facebook." Smarty Pant pointed to her napkin. "We did too. It doesn't add up." Matt said, "They wait until I read the scores before sharing the clue." He seemed excited to be saying it out loud. "They get their bonus points after I read the scores. That's why no one knows how to bet against them." Smarty Pant said, "Isn't that…. Cheating?" Matt said, "I never said *when* you have to share the clue to get your points." I said, "Look weak when strong, strong when weak. Sun Tzu, Art of War." I was trying to be jokey but she looked crestfallen. She said, "I only joined Facebook in the first place to get those points." She left the napkin on Matt's table when she walked out.

Streets were kind of empty when I drove to the bowling alley tonight. Just Daryl, Jack, and me at the corner of the bar in classic B2 formation. Spare Time felt more like a library than a bowling alley, people kept their heads down and murmured to one another. Lots of empty tables and not much crosstalk from team to team. Fewer pin crashings from the bowling alley. Got a text on the university emergency thread which said spring break has been extended by one week to give them more time to figure things out. Name a type of open air mine which gets its name from the Latin word for square. We can't spell Kyrgyzstan. We don't know how many pounds within one the average cremated human body weighs. Jack had a sixty pound dog and his cremains weighed about 5lbs, so we guessed 15 pounds for a human which turned out to not even be close. We're off our game all night, even missing the Facebook clue, "What is the color associated with the Virgin Mary?" It's Marian Blue, not a color any of us had heard of. I had Googled the clue but we still missed it. The sports TV over the bar flashed news that basketball had been suspended; not just the game, but all the games. The entire season. We didn't win and I can't remember what place we came in. On the way home, the radio said Tom Hanks and his wife have it. I told Molly about that when I got back but she had already heard.

Bappa Came By

A be McNair drove up in the Gator. He said, "Is Hercules here?"

He had caught a raccoon in a Have-a-Heart trap and driven the animal out to the old cemetery in the overgrown timber a few miles down West Grove to release it. After letting the raccoon go, he had backed into one of the large tombstones and knocked it over. "That's what I get for having a heart." Now he wanted Ben to drive out with him and lift the tombstone back into position. Ben was mid-workout, but he was gracious and put on a shirt and headed out in the Gator with his grandpa. There had been some concern about Abe driving the Gator these days, but against doctors' orders he was still operating all the farm equipment, even the tractors and bulldozers.

They returned an hour later. I was outside with a beer and peanuts, reading up on the Route 66 bike route I wanted to someday pedal. Abe sat on the lawn chair next to me and took some peanuts. Natty had been monitoring his diet so when she wasn't around, a salty peanut was irresistible. Abe did turn down a beer—he wasn't feeling that brave. He smelled not unpleasantly of machine oil and perspiration. He said he and Ben had not been able to do it. "We just just needed one more strong guy to lift that tombstone. Three of us could have gotten it right." He didn't mean me: Abe had lifted weights most of his life just as Ben did these days; he meant another strong guy like that.

Later Ben told me, "We just needed two strong guys. Bappa can't lift anything anymore."

Molly, Ben, Madeleine and I drove to Abe and Natty's for dinner. Caspian was back from work and joined us. He was staying in their basement and working with the Hoogler Forest Preserve to earn money before going back to Northland College in Wisconsin. The "Summer of Caspian" was in full swing. We ate chicken, hog-rotten potatoes, salad, and corn bread.

Abe knocked over his iced tea. As Natty mopped the spill with a rag, she said it reminded her of a time when the cousins were little, and Abe had spilled his drink twice at one meal. She said, "Maggie had just started kindergarten and when he spilled the second time, she yelled, 'Look! Bappa did it again!'"

At this meal, a short while later, Abe knocked over his iced tea a second time and Madeleine said, "Look! Bappa did it again!" We all laughed and Natty took Abe's plate and replaced his tea soaked salad. No one laughed later when Abe reached for the pitcher and spilled for the third time.

Molly and I fought about the Muck boots. She was wearing mine and because I could not fit my feet in her Mucks, I had to take two from the old, mismatched pile. The left boot had a crack and leaked, but we were just walking to the barnyard anyway, not across the creek so it didn't matter.

As we got to the bottom of the hill to check the mailbox, the Gator pulled up. Caspian was driving, helping Abe with chores. In about twenty seconds, Caspian told us about some trees he was going to cut, a mountain bike trail he wanted to clear, a bike ride he wanted to take to Augustana to see his brother Noel, and prairie grass he was going to plant after he did a "controlled burn" on the hillside along our driveway. Molly and I just listened and nodded.

Abe said Natty had gotten hit by a car this morning. We were startled, but he said she just got a small scrape on her arm. This had been at a reception for a new ag program at the Senior Center. Jim Everet, the veterinarian, had been at the event and had checked Natty's injury.

I said, "And then he dewormed and castrated her."

No one laughed.

Molly said, "How is mom doing?"

Abe said she was fine, she was already driving to the Dig n' Save to get cheap appliances for Maggie's dorm room, despite Maggie having not yet begun applying to schools.

Natty had always been singularly dedicated to her grandchildren; focused on them to the exclusivity of everything else. One of my best jokes was about the time when Natty got kicked by a horse, which she had muzzled to prevent from overeating. After a few days of being hungry, Bay Boy had wheeled around and kicked Natty in the chest, busting her ribcage and puncturing a lung. Natty had managed to crawl across the pasture and pull herself up against a fence post to flag down a passing car for help. My joke was that, when she finally managed to get the driver's attention, she said, "Caspian got a soccer scholarship at Northland College and I've just been kicked by a horse!"

Molly and I went to Carlyle for a beer while waiting for Madeleine to finish her cello lesson. We sat in the booth with the trapezoid table at the picture window. It was still overcast but the sky was brightening. I got a Humulus and she had the walnut stout. Molly had the idea that we should each say something that made us happy.

We took a minute, but it was easy for me. I said, "The bicycle. You changed my life."

When Molly had sold her first short story, she took the money and bought a bicycle for me: a Trek hybrid with a carbon fork, lightyears ahead of anything I had ever pedaled before. This was almost 20 years ago, but she had opened a whole world for me. We had moved to the farm, were living where she grew up, and I had felt like a permanent outsider. Through riding the bike I made great friends and become part of a community. Pedaling country roads had given me an appreciation for the landscape and led me to take an interest in doing more on the farm. Really, she had given me two families: first hers and then ours. I got teary trying to explain how her gift had changed me.

I said, "It's like you gave me a universe. And then with the bike, you gave me the tool I needed to find my place in the world." I was spinning the cardboard coaster to keep myself from full on weeping.

Molly said, "That's sweet."

The thing that made her happy was the shape of Sophie's head. She called it "boxy and comforting," a perfect dog-head shape.

The plan was for us to get Madeleine and then the three of us would get dinner somewhere, maybe pick up the boys and get wings at Chili Pepper, but we got a call from Natty that Abe was acting strange. He was sitting in the car and wouldn't get out of the passenger seat. He was blinking and breathing but not speaking and would not move his legs. She and Caspian couldn't lift him, so they called an ambulance. We picked up Madeleine and headed home. On Highway Two we drove by the ambulance which was taking Abe to Rockford Memorial.

Molly asked Madeleine and me to come visit her in the hospital while she was sitting bedside with her dad. She also wanted us to bring her lunch, a cheeseburger from Beefaroo because it was near the hospital. Before hanging up, she added fries and a chocolate milkshake. When I told Madeleine what Molly's order was, she said, "Oh no! Poor mom."

I drove into Rockford to see Abe in rehab. Natty and Molly had been going every day but asked me to go today because they were "doing" the farm books with the accountant (whom they like because "he rescues dogs," and has a basket of snack sized chips in his waiting room. They don't eat any, but Natty takes some home for Caspian.)

Man Vatre Rehab was long and sprawling, like it was

built wing by wing without a masterplan. I was able to wander around unmolested and found Abe in the cafeteria eating breakfast.

"There he is," he said. I was worried he would be disappointed to see it was me who had come, but that didn't seem to be the case. He was wearing a hoodie from Noel's school and green sweatpants. We had a nice chat and he introduced me to some of the other inmates. Instead of saying I was his son-in-law, he said, "This is Dan. He's a good man, and there's darn few of us left." This was a standard joke of his, something he said when introducing people but couldn't remember anything else about them.

A physical therapist in hospital scrubs was the last person he introduced, and the three of us walked to the workout area, where she had him step up and down standalone stairs. Abe held on to both rails and walked five steps up to the top, then went backwards five steps down. It took a long time. "You're leaning forward, Abe," the therapist said to him. She radiated confidence. "Don't look down at your feet." She told me her father and grandfather knew Abe. Her dad had been on the football team in high school. She said all the parents who were farmers trusted Abe with their kids because he never pushed too hard; as a farmer himself, he knew the unique work stress on kids from family farms.

While Abe carefully worked the stairs, I looked around at some of the other people in the facility. Most were older, but some were my age, and some were younger. They worked in pairs, rolling balls to one another, swinging their arms in patterns, holding batons steady. They worked with such concentration and deliberation you couldn't help but feel that the key to life is just to move as much as possible. Getting around is actually the thing you would miss the most if you couldn't do it: not food or sex or sleeping. It isn't the caffeine you love in your coffee, it's the ability to reach over and get it yourself. I decided then and there I would absolutely do that bike ride in the summer no matter what. I wrote in my green, pocket notebook, "Resolved: this summer, I will load up the Salsa Marrake$h bike and pedal to my mother's house in New Mexico. I will use RT 66 when I can. It will take three weeks, rain or shine, headwinds or flat tires, eleven hundred miles, fully self-sustained and self supported, from my garage to my mother's front door." I signed and wrote the date.

Abe was tired but when we went back to his room, two nurses came in and took him to the bathroom to change his clothes and clean him up a little. I could hear him talking to the nurses while they bathed him. He seemed to be having a nice time. Abe asked if they knew

Josh Gilliford. They didn't, so he filled them in. Abe said, Josh was a physician's assistant who used to work for a doctor here at Man Vatre, but Josh and the doctor had a falling out, which is why he and his wife moved to Montana. Missoula. Abe said, Josh's wife was a yoga teacher just like his daughter, and that was how he knew him. Josh bow hunted on the farm when he lived here. Josh had once lost his sunglasses in our "spring-fed lake" and Abe explained how he had gotten a wetsuit and spent a day diving and looking for those sunglasses, but never did find them. He said he missed seeing Josh around the farm during hunting season.

When they emerged from the bathroom Abe seemed confused to see me. He said to the nurses, "This is… Dan. He's a good man, and there's darned few of us left."

Before dinner, Natty drove Abe over to look at the baby chicks. Madeleine showed them the chirping tub under the heat lamp in our garage. Abe seemed unsteady and had apparently fallen earlier in the day, but he was engaged and held a few of the yellow ones in his hand. We had stir fry for dinner but Natty wouldn't let Abe have any of the sauce because she said it was too salty. For dessert he was given half a cookie. When Natty turned her back, Abe pointed to the cookie tray and I gave him the other half.

Natty said Hank was going to bring on some high school kids to help cut hay this year.

Abe sighed. He said, "I'll be well enough to run the tractor when it's time to bale. "

Natty and I exchanged glances. I knew she was hiding all the tractor and harvester keys. It seemed to be Abe's singular goal to get up on a farm machine once again.

We played a round of Oh Hell and I did pretty well for the first rounds, then badly from there on out and finished mid-pack. Natty won. She said, "Oh Bappa, look at this! You have 53 points! That's just eleven below me."

Caspian came over to watch soccer in our basement. He took a beer and told me they had seen Sophie chasing one of the the chickens, and that Abe had swatted her on the snout with a glove. Sophie responded by rolling on to her back for a tum-rub and Abe knelt down and gave her one. As a result, Caspian didn't think Sophie had gotten the message about not chasing chickens.

The Mucks were in disarray again, and I took two random boots and walked down the hill to the barnyard to feed the horses. Abe was sitting in the driver's seat of the Gator, idling near the dumpster. He was talking to our neighbor, Lars Dryturd. Lars was leaning against his car with his arms crossed and both he and Abe waved. I reflexively reached to my back pocket for my checkbook. Despite being our nearest neighbor, the only time I saw Lars was when the Dryturds were fundraising for their kid's homeschool programs or when they drove over with a pamphlet for me, such as last year's "From Meaningless to Messiah: One Jew's Journey to Salvation."

I went to the barn. Abe had already fed the horses and he had left the gate open to their pen. I closed it and decided not to say anything, though I wondered how he had gotten the keys to the Gator. I got a Busch Lite from the farmer's fridge in the pole barn and walked over to where Lars and Abe were chatting. Lars' head was like a giant, bland honeydew melon with a bushy moustache. I thought this would be a good a time to congratulate him on his victory over me for township Commissioner, but as I approached, he got back in his car.

He was saying to Abe, "Well, just stopped by because I was feeling neighborly." He paused, then asked if he could borrow the John Deere on Monday. Abe said that would be fine. When Lars left Abe said, "You chorin'? I already fed the horses. Those my boots?"

I held up my left foot. "Just this one."

Abe and Natty came for dinner. It was dark already but Molly had the porchlight going to make it easier for them to walk on the uneven flagstones. Madeleine was working on her cello in her bedroom and Natty went into the kitchen for a glass of wine and ice. Abe settled on the couch near me and my laptop. He said, "What are you working on?"

I showed him my route for the bike trip on Rt 66. He looked at the map with the 1,100 mile route highlighted. I let him see my list of possible camp sites. I also showed him the list of breweries and burrito places I was compiling. Abe scanned the maps and I took out my phone and posted a HeyBeerCat photo on Instagram and listened to Natty talk about how Maggie was going to Houston during her gap year and how Bridget was going to drop her off at the airport in St. Louis and then go to Trader Joe's. She also said Sam had gotten a haircut and a girlfriend and now that Caspian was back at Northland College, Noel would be moving into their basement next week.

Abe picked up a James Baldwin book Molly was using in her class. He said, "Now this is a classic!"

Natty said, "Who is that? He was mentioned in a poem the Rodgers gave us." Apparently Martin Rodgers has been passing around a bit of web-trash; a parody poem about Trump based on Green Eggs and Ham. Natty said, "It's something about how Trump hates James Baldwin. Who is James Baldwin?"

I said, "Was it maybe Alec Baldwin?"

Natty said, "Oh yes! So who is Alec Baldwin?"

I could not put off cleaning the chicken coop any longer, so I readied my farmer costume: the blue overalls and bandana around my face to keep from inhaling chicken poop. Molly will occasionally remind me that I am a product of the suburbs: that I spent my youth refusing to leave the car during picnics for fear of insects and not swimming in the manmade lake in my subdivision if I saw algae on the surface. Even now when I do my "chores," I feel like an imposter, so getting the look right is important. The only giveaway detail was my Muck boots were missing, but I used an old pair of Abe's which were a size too big and made me walk funny.

I pitchforked the old straw, ossified turds and all, on to the manure spreader, which Abe's farming partner Hank had left for me by the coop. The manure spreader—a long trough on wheels—had an adjustable conveyer belt with teeth so the dirty straw could be spread evenly along the ground when it was towed behind a tractor.

In the barnyard, I got two new bales of straw with the Gator and drove them up the hill to the coop. I spread the new straw on the ground and in the nests. Then I drove the Gator back down and looked for someone to drive the tractor and hook it up to the manure spreader. Abe was in the pole barn sorting nails into coffee cans. He said Hank and Jakob had both gone for the day, but he could show me how to use the tractor. Because I wouldn't be able to close the coop until the manure spreader was moved, I took him up on it.

He led me past the full sized John Deere to the smaller International tractor, which he called, "Red Johnny." Red Johnny didn't have a cab, just a single seat between the oversized tires. It had a steering wheel with a brodie knob and an open dash with a set of three gear shifts like on a manual transmission car: one for speed, one to raise and lower the bucket, and another that had something to do with the power belt, which controlled whatever machine the tractor was pulling at the moment; a mower blade or a hay tedder or, in this case, the manure spreader.

Abe talked me through going forward and starting and stopping. "There's a lot going on there, so if you get confused a minute, just stop and look and go slow. It's always okay to slow down to figure things out."

Starting Red Johnny was tricky. One had to turn the key and pull the choke out and hit the pedal with just the right amount of pressure. After a few failed tries where the tractor sputtered or just made grinding noises, Abe said it would be easier if he did it himself. I climbed down off the seat and Abe got up. I kept my hand pressed on his back when he seemed to be leaning backward too far on the platform, but he got himself situated on the seat. He seemed happy but played it cool. It took him a few tries too, but eventually there was a hesitant rumble from the machine and the motor turned over.

Abe shouted over the noise of the engine. "I'll drive it out of the pole barn." When I didn't answer he yelled, "If you're worried, you can stand on the platform and hang on. You can always pull the choke and the tractor will just shut off." This didn't sound right, but I climbed up and stood on the steps and hung on the grab-bar beside the chair.

He was confident and went slow. Like this, we left the pole barn, crossed the road, went past the mailbox and headed up the hill to the chicken coop to spread the manure.

Grey and drizzly morning. Noticed my shower door repair, which I intended to include in my June Wins—my signal achievement for the month—had broken again. The castors were no longer rolling in the track. Went out to open the coop but the hens were already scattered in the yard. It had been dark when I closed the door last night and I hadn't noticed they weren't in. The chickens had probably roosted in the trees all night. I swung the door open and found a sleeping animal curled up warmly in the corner, furry body rising and falling with gentle snores. Seemed to be exactly what Molly described yesterday, but she said her dad had come and shot it. While I looked for the pitchfork, Abe happened to drive by in the Gator toward the fields. I told him we had a possum in the coop.

He said, "Yesterday I shot it but forgot to go back and check."

I didn't mind possums or raccoons really, except they kill chickens and smash their eggs. Raising chickens means taking a side. The racoons don't even eat the chickens, they just rip their heads off and leave the bodies on the ground, terrorizing the birds and leaving a mess for me.

I waited for Abe to come back, watching the ducks wander down the hill all the way toward the creek. They really loved the light rain. When I got done checking the water for the grass-fat cows, the chickens were still very agitated, not going near their food or their nests to lay eggs. The possum was still in the corner and Abe had not returned. I was about to get the pitchfork and try to move the possum along, but Abe came back with a pistol. I asked if that gun was big enough for the job. He said it was.

As we approached, the possum uncurled, and opened its mouth and hissed. In that position, it was significantly less cute, which maybe made it easier for me to watch Abe pop him in the head. The animal started flipping around in the straw.

Abe said, "That's what he did last time. That's the fifth shot I put in him."

The possum was bleeding from the wound but not from anywhere else so I thought it was probably a different animal. I found a metal pail in the garage and heard him fire the gun a second time. Abe lifted the possum by the tail and dropped him into the bucket. When I unchained the gate for him, Abe drove off toward the creek.

Molly called. She was parked by her parents mailbox and said her dad was in the ditch in the Gator. She had been driving home and found him like that on the side of the road. I got in the car and drove over just as Noel also pulled up, coming home from his job at Skrotum McBinch Carpentry.

Abe was in good spirits. He said he slipped off the

side of the road and had just been waiting for someone to find him. It took all three of us to get him free, mostly because Abe wasn't moving his limbs. I was pulling him by his belt loops and Noel and Molly were each under one arm. For his part, Abe thought this was all pretty funny. Once we got him out of the ditch he took a few steps on his own and sat down in Noel's car. We gave him a bottle of water and he drank it easily.

He pointed to my Mucks. "I thought those didn't fit you."

I said, "I put insoles in them! They're really comfortable now. I actually like them better than my own boots," and I pointed to my boots on Molly's feet.

Abe said. "I'm going to need them back when we cut hay next week. I'm driving the combine."

Molly and I joined the others on Natty's screened-in porch where a guy named Bob, described as a friend and a "pastor," came to get stories about Abe for the eulogy. Bridget and Lemmy were there, and so were most of the cousins. Pastor Bob was tall and did a lot of grinning. He sipped a soft drink and said, "It must be nice living so close to a golf course."

No one really responded to that.

Pastor Bob took notes but not many. I had that nervous feeling one gets when the waiter isn't writing down your order. We told our anecdotes, how Molly and I once took Abe to an Irish bar in Chicago and Lemmy recounted asking permission from Abe before proposing to Bridget. Pastor Bob nodded a lot, as if every anecdote just confirmed his long standing belief about what a great guy Abe was. After a story from Natty about Abe and Martin Rodgers playing practical jokes on each other, Pastor Bob said it reminded him of how, "kids like jokes." He said he knew one about a hippopotamus and a brother and a sister. "One of them stood behind the hippo while the other, either the brother or the sister, took off their shoes and waited." Then he kind of trailed off. He continued nodding until Natty asked him if he wanted a refill on his soft drink. He did.

Molly and Noel went along on the Hop-On ride just to have something to do in the days leading up to the funeral. I set up the bikes: made sure the tires were inflated, lubed the chains, put a Cliff bar in all the saddle bags. Then three of us drove to the White Pelican launch site and waited for Dom and the Hop-On bus to New Glarus.

Caspian met us in New Glarus with the farm truck, which he had apparently taken up to Northland. He had his bike with him, so all four of us were able to ride. I understood the trip to be 12 miles one way, making it a 24 mile round trip, just barely in the range of being worthwhile; but it turned out Monticello was six miles away on the bike path from New Glarus. Twelve miles was the round trip. I apologized to Caspian and Noel and they were nice about it. Dom was hauling a cooler in the tagalong behind his bike, and we drank two or three beers as we went along. When we got to Sugar River Pizza we started ordering by the pitcher. We sat at the big table with the Hop-On crew and one of the women asked Molly if the boys were our sons.

Molly said, "Nephews."

I said, "We do have children but we don't take them out with us."

Because Molly had one beer the entire afternoon, she drove the truck home and Caspian took the bus with Noel and me. Molly had my phone for some reason and I had hers. I can't remember why. Easier for Molly to use directions on my phone maybe? I bought a case of Moon Man for the bus ride and they were all gone when we got back to Scoldin.

When I woke up at 6:30am the next morning, Molly was furious. She had discovered I had texted Megan her yoga sequence with her phone. I remembered copying it from her notes and texting them, but couldn't remember why I thought that would be funny. She pointed out that the text was in response to Megan checking on her. That Megan had written, "Thinking of you. How is your family doing?" And I had responded as Molly, "Urdhva uttanasana, ardha parivrtta, prasarita padottanasana, trikonasana, bhujangasana, marichyasana D variation."

I agreed it was tasteless and not funny and that I would text Megan to apologize.

We sat up front, jammed in two pews. The first hymn was the Penn Sunday School theme so that was kind of fun. Then Caspian read his thing which was brief and well done. He cited Abe as the reason he was interested in nature, and by extension, the world. He vowed to live a conscientious, sustainable life, in honor of his Bappa.

Then grinning Pastor Bob came on. He started his eulogy by describing Abe as a young man. "Picture Rory McIlroy," he said. "Ruddy cheeks and curly blonde hair, that's what Abe looked like too." Then he talked about his many accomplishments. Not Abe's, Rory McIlroy's. Pastor Bob told us Rory McIlroy was one of the youngest golfers to ever earn a million dollars in a single season. He said, "Doesn't that sound like the kind of spirit Abe had?"

Eh, maybe. But Abe never played golf, never talked about golf or watched it on television. In fact the only time he ever mentioned the game was when he talked about his irritation with having a golf course abut the farm.

"Rory has not won a Masters Tournament yet," Pastor Bob continued. "Rory is a true competitor and won't give up until he has achieved every milestone golf has to offer." Pastor Bob seemed to get choked up. "You can count on Rory," he whispered, and overcome with emotion, he stepped back from the rostrum and took a moment to compose himself.

After a sip of water, Pastor Bob began with the anecdotes, which he predictably botched. It was Molly and Lemmy who had taken Abe to the Irish bar, and I was the one who asked for permission to wed Bridget. Then Pastor Bob began listing Abe's failures: that it had taken him six colleges to get his teaching degree, and how his record as Hawks football coach wasn't especially remarkable.

These were things we had told Pastor Bob, and they were basically true. Failure was something Abe often joked about, but somehow to have it all catalogued when Abe wasn't around to share in the laugh felt mean. And Pastor Bob never said the other part: Yes, Abe didn't have a winning record as a football coach, but his players revered him because he was kind and forgiving. Yes, Abe often came in late for supper, but it was because he enjoyed being on the farm doing things. If the sun was shining, he wanted to be out working. He never wanted a day to end.

Finally Pastor Bob wrapped it up by telling us, "Abraham McNair found Christ" through his love for Natty and that Natty had led him to "minister students" as a guidance counselor. This dubious third act stunner was shocking news to many of us at the funeral, but I did at least feel a little sympathy for Pastor Bob. Endings are tough, and people really respond to a good ol' redemptive love story. I had to admit it: Pastor Bob had stuck the landing.

Postscript: transcribed from handwritten notes from my green pocket diary, Buffalo Wild Wings, Peru, IL.

I'll start @ the end. I was eager then dismayed & then knew I would quit in Tulsa and take the train back. Once I decided that, it seemed silly to go even that far & I should quit in Joplin, and then a few minutes later, St Louis seemed like long enough. Then I decided to quit when I got to Springfield. I had shaved two and a half weeks off the trip and I hadn't even made it to lunch. Got a sandwich at a grocery store and told the cashier I was riding my bike down RT 66, but I already knew I wasn't even going to make it *to* RT 66.

Afternoon got hotter and head-windy. Drank a gallon of water at a gas station by Interstate 80 and bought a Chapstick. Pedaled another eight miles until my back wheel got soft. Flipped the bike in the only shady spot I could find, a small tree in front of a farmhouse. Dog barking inside but I don't think anyone was home. Lost the valve converter in the grass and realized I had not brought a second. Deflated the tube & pulled it out of the tire. It already had two patches—why didn't I start with a new tube? Stupid stupid! Put the spare into the wheel and inflated it with the air canister but the tube popped like a birthday balloon. I only had one more spare in my bag, so I inflated it slowly with the frame pump. Tube held, but I couldn't get the pump head seated right so I only got it to useable instead of full. I no longer believed I could/would make it even to Eureka tonight. I called Molly and asked her if she would pick me up. She said, "Really?" I had been gone seven hours.

Pedaled back to Peru and locked the bike and sat at the bar inside the Buffalo Wild Wings. I told the bartender, "I was supposed to bike to New Mexico, eleven hundred miles, but I only did 86 miles and now I'm quitting."

She was sweet, supportive. I was her only customer, just the two of us under a dozen large screen televisions. She said, "If your friends give you shit about quitting, you tell them none of them could go 86 miles in one day."

This isn't actually true of my friends but I took her point, partially because she kind of had an Emma Stone thing going and partially because she said my first beer was on her, which she pulled from the Pabst tap and then walked away.

It's funny how failure seems like it's the worst thing in the world in the abstract, but then when you actually fail at something it just seems like it was always going to be that way and not even that big of a deal. I was going home instead of biking RT 66, but I like being on the farm. There are chores to do, chickens to feed, eggs to collect, dogs to walk, cat boxes to clean, grass to cut. There will be leaves to rake and wood to split and snow to plow, and there are lots of bike rides I can take close to home, where I can have dinner with my family at night and sleep in my own bed and make my own coffee in the morning.

I pinged Molly's phone and saw she was still a half hour away. I signaled for another beer, and waited for Molly to come rescue me.

DAN LIBMAN is the author of the short story collection *Married But Looking*. He is a past winner of a Pushcart Prize and a Paris Review Discovery Prize (now called the Plimpton Prize.) His fiction and essays have been widely published and anthologized, and he is a regular on-air contributor to WNIJ, Northern Public Radio. Libman lives on a family farm in Illinois with his wife, the writer Molly McNett, their two kids, three cats, a dog, and dozens of chickens. He blogs occasionally for the website thecompleterist.com.

9 781959 556404